DEATH BY NIGHT

THE DEPARTMENT Z SERIES

The Death Miser

Redhead

First Came a Murder

Death Round the Corner

The Mark of the Crescent

Thunder in Europe

The Terror Trap

Carriers of Death

Days of Danger

Death Stands By

Menace

Murder Must Wait

Panic!

Death by Night

The Island of Peril

Sabotage

Go Away Death

The Day of Disaster

Prepare for Action

No Darker Crime

Dark Peril

The Peril Ahead

The League of Dark Men

The Department of Death

The Enemy Within

Dead or Alive

A Kind of Prisoner

The Black Spiders

DEATH BY NIGHT

DEPARTMENT Z

JOHN CREASEY

OPEN ROAD

INTEGRATED MEDIA

NEW YORK

ISBN: 978-1-5040-9213-5

This edition published in 2024 by Open Road Integrated Media, Inc.
180 Maiden Lane
New York, NY 10038
www.openroadmedia.com

DEATH BY NIGHT

1

TWO GENTLEMEN RETURN

From the Boat Train at Waterloo stepped two large, weary-looking men who created the impression that for some time past they had slept in their clothes. Nor was the impression unjustified, for it was precisely five nights since they had known the luxury of a bed. Even then the bed had been a single one, and they were broad as well as tall, each used to four feet of spring-interior mattress, blankets and luxury eiderdown. To them it seemed that such amenities were never likely to return, for Waterloo Station, with the dim, blue gleams from the lamps hanging from the glass roof, and the bookstalls, was a place of gloom. Vague figures walked past them in either direction.

On the roof pattered heavy rain, while it was piercing cold.

'I am not,' said Mark Errol, 'going another step without a porter. Unless you would like to carry my bag.'

'If you carry me, it's a deal.' Michael Errol stifled a yawn, and tried to pierce the gloom—unsuccessfully. He felt too tired even to exchange witticisms with his cousin. 'Oh, well, we can't stay here all night. What's the time?'

'Just after nine.'

'Half an hour late,' reflected Michael; 'it might have been worse. I—porter. *Porter!*'

'Coming, sir!'

A weedy figure materialised, revealing a wizened face decorated with a wispish moustache. The man jumped into the carriage and pulled down two small suit-cases. The two large men eyed him as they would any phenomenon.

'Two trunks in the van, porter,' Mark said.

'Aye, aye, sir, I'll just get a truck. Got your name on?'

'Errol. Put them all in a taxi, and tell the cabby to wait; we're going to have a drink. And,' went on Mike, passing over a pound note, 'tell him he may have to wait a long time.'

'All okey-doke, sir.' The porter disappeared towards the luggage van, whistling tunelessly. The Errols walked stiffly towards the gates, their eyes lack-lustre and their mouths dry. The sweeping Errol chin which characterised them was not entirely hidden by the gloom; nor were their claims to handsomeness, for they were impressive young men, each topping the six foot mark, each turning the scales at fourteen stone, each possessed of the Errol cleft in the chin but minus the Errol Roman nose. Their noses were straight. Their eyes were grey and fringed with long lashes, their hair dark brown—Mark's straight and well-brushed, Mike's unruly— and that their clothes, although untidy, were from Savile Row.

They were oblivious of those about them as they went towards the buffet—but two people, one a short man with a Punch of a chin and a beaked nose, approached them from one side.

The second man was taller, and very thin.

Again the light prevented strangers from seeing the swarthiness of his skin, and the unpleasant closeness of his eyes. He sidled, and sidling out-walked the short man, and drew alongside the Errols.

'Excuse me, gentlemen...'

His voice was low-pitched, and possessed a note that did not sound English. The Errols stopped with one accord. Mark, who did most of the talking, raised a brow.

'Yes?'

'I've brought a message from Mr. Loftus, gentlemen.'

The close-set eyes were narrow, but that might have been because of trying to see through the black-out. Had the Errols disliked all they could see of the stranger, their immediate uncertainties would have been removed, for the name of Loftus was virtually a password.

They liked to think that they were useful agents of that remarkable organisation called Department Z, but it often appeared that Loftus and others took all the plums, and that if there was a job where it was impossible to triumph, Loftus— Agent Number 1—handed it to them. Certainly he was not popular with them at that moment. All they wanted was drink and food and sleep.

'We do not know a Mr. Loftus,' stated Mark clearly.

'I—I beg pardon, sir?'

'You heard,' said Mark, and then resignedly: 'All right. Where is he?'

'In the booking-hall, sir, in the corner on the left. He doesn't want to be seen contacting with you.'

'Hmm,' said Mark. 'All right, whoever-you-are, lead the way, will you?'

'Yes, sir.'

The thin man of the furtive face led the way, and behind the trio followed he of the Punch-like chin. The station was not crowded, and yet they contrived to bump into several people.

The shadows of the booking-hall engulfed them. Peering across, they saw no figure lurking in the left corner, but the darkness might deliver anyone up at a moment's notice. Approaching the corner, the thin man fell behind.

There was a sharp cry from behind them, and on the instant they came to a standstill.

'Mark—be careful!'

Then the thin man moved.

He snatched something from his pocket which showed a dull glint and then the something went flying from his grasp, for Mike Errol forgot weariness and moved. He leapt at the man, crashing a clenched right fist towards his stomach, and the man doubled up; a gun fell from nerveless fingers. Mike struck again, a left swing this time to the chin. The furtive one's feet lifted inches from the ground and he went backwards like a pole-axed bull.

Mike drew a deep breath.

'Now that,' he said, 'is what I call a warm welcome. Hallo, Spats, nice of you to come to meet us. What's the matter?'

Spats Thornton, one of Craigie's most useful agents since he did not look like one, put one hand in his pocket and contemplated the Errols with his chin jutting out.

'You're the matter,' said he dispassionately. 'I heard every word, and you fell for it.'

'So it seems,' said Mike ruefully. 'But we can go into that later. Here are two men wearily returning from Italy after a damn' fool journey, and the moment we get back to London someone draws a gun on us. I want to know why.' He did not sound over-curious, for he had worked with the Department too long to be surprised at anything.

Mark stooped down and picked up the gun.

It was a Webley automatic, and the safety-catch had not been released. Not that a shot would have caused much disturbance, for the small snout of its improved Maxim silencer poked from the muzzle.

'If he'd fired,' said Mark more dreamily than his wont, 'it would have been death in darkness and no mistake. What and who is he, Spats?'

'I haven't a notion. I noticed him come up to you and heard about the message from Loftus.'

'Good Lord!' exclaimed Mike, and he seemed positively enlivened. 'There wasn't a message, we can have that drink! Look after this little çago, Spats; if I don't lower something...'

'Silence,' said Spats Thornton.

There were occasions when he could make his voice sound sepulchral, and it did then. There were folk who claimed that he always seemed to be putting on an act, and in a measure that was true. It was equally true of most of the Department men, for they worked in a world where little was natural, where death lurked in every corner, where it was impossible to know from one moment to the next what was going to happen. Living like that, they developed an unseen armour of what some called humour. It was a peculiar brand, mingling sarcasm with facetiousness, and it puzzled folk who did not know them well.

'All right,' said Mike, 'we're silent.'

'What really puzzles me,' said Spats, rubbing his chin, 'is how he knew that there was a message. Bill wants to see you at once and I've come to meet you. Someone else knew you were going to be here, and the someone doesn't want you. If you want a drink there's just time for it. I've got a cab.'

'What about that?' demanded Mike, nodding towards the man on the ground.

'I'll watch it,' said Spats. 'Go and get rid of your repressions.'

The Errols walked towards the buffet. There was a certain

7

humour in the fact that they had been sent out on a quest which had carried them through most of Southern Europe where they might have expected excitement, and the first sign of trouble had come at the moment of their return to London.

Drinking, they considered the mystery of the fact that someone knew that they had been due at Waterloo on the 8.37 (arrival) train.

From Southampton they had sent a telegram to Bill Loftus, announcing their impending arrival, and to their knowledge no one else in England knew that they had landed. Therefore, it seemed, the leakage was through Loftus.

'Ye-es,' admitted Mark. 'Well, let's get back.' He yawned, lit a cigarette—Mark refusing—and they strolled back towards the booking-hall. The gloom and the ghostly blue light remained. Thornton lurked in the darkness, and the man remained on the floor.

'Our friend still sleeps,' said Spats, but he smiled, 'which one of you hit him?'

'I,' said Mike with satisfaction. 'We'd better get him round; they'll see us carrying him to a cab even in this. Whisky?'

Spats drew a flask from his hip pocket, adjusted the knee of his trousers, and knelt down. Unscrewing the top of the flask, he held it to the man's lip, and a trickle of whisky forced itself through.

'He can't be as bad as that,' he said almost irritably, while the Errols stood and peered down. 'Wake up, you lump of sin, or—*God!*'

He straightened up, spilling whisky over the dusty platform, where it ran in little globules. Mark replaced him—and Mike also bent down, to see the small hole in the man's temple, the little trickle of blood coming from it.

The man had been shot while Thornton had been on guard.

2

CRAIGIE AND OTHERS

I 've been standing here all the time, and I heard nothing and saw nothing,' Thornton said. 'It's fantastic, but I've fallen down on the job.'

'Did you have any idea that there'd be one?' demanded Michael.

'I knew something was in the wind,' said Thornton, and he shrugged his shoulders. 'Stay here. I'll go to phone Bill Loftus, he may have some ideas about the body.'

The Errols stayed. In each man's mind there was the thought that if the dead man had been shot in the darkness, the same thing could happen to them. It was not a comforting thought but nor was it worrying.

Thornton was returning from the telephone kiosk when Mark spoke for the first time.

'Something,' he said, 'is up.'

'I'm glad,' said Mike sarcastically, 'that you've reached that conclusion so soon.'

Thornton materialised and spoke briefly.

'The Yard's contacting with the station police. We're to

wait until officials arrive and then to Brook Street as quickly as we can. I hope they're not long; my cab's waiting.'

Mike stared.

'Cab...?'

'Cab!' exclaimed Mark, and for the first time since the discovery of murder he grinned. 'There's another cab and a porter waiting somewhere; we're not going to be very popular. I'll go to locate 'em, Mike.'

'Better have the stuff taken to the flat,' advised Mike.

Mark went off, and located his cabby, and the attendant porter. The cabby's reception was not in the first instance polite. Mark, at times prepared to humour anyone from a cabby to a king, did not feel in that mood just then.

'That's enough,' he said sharply. 'You were told to wait and you're waiting. Get this stuff to 55g, Brook Street. My man will take it in and pay you.'

'Very good, sir.' A subdued cabby let in the clutch and started off, while the wizened-faced porter disappeared, as if afraid that the pound he had received already would be demanded from him. Mark remarked to himself that there would have to be an improvement to his temper. He...

'Oh, I'm so sorry!'

The voice was feminine. It was warm, it had a musical note, was low-pitched and could be called husky. One of the loveliest voices. Its owner had banged into Mark and was recoiling backwards; in the gloom behind her Mark could pick out the outlines of a suit-case, and she was liable to fall over it. He stretched out a hand swiftly, gripped her wrist, and pulled her towards him.

'My fault,' he said; in the half-light and at close quarters he seemed a remarkably handsome man. 'Are you allright?'

'Yes, thanks.' He could see enough to tell that she was in furs which were caught together at the neck, that she was neither short nor tall, and that what part of her face was visible beneath the nose-length veil she was wearing seemed to match her voice. 'It's impossible in the dark, isn't it, and I was trying to catch the nine-twelve.'

'Too bad,' said Mark; 'it's turned nine-thirty.'

'What?'

She seemed so startled that immediately he took pity on her. She pulled back the cuff of her coat, and with the help of a small torch fastened to her wrist, saw that her watch pointed to nine-fifteen. Mark's watch made it twenty-five to ten, and she looked at him in mingled self-annoyance and disappointment.

'Twenty minutes slow, and I've been hurrying...' She broke off. 'Well, that means staying in Town overnight, and I'll have to telephone.'

'I can show you the kiosks,' said Mark promptly.

'No, I mustn't detain you any longer.'

'I'm insisting.' said Mark cheerfully.

She laughed again, and with more humour, and he wished that the line of telephone kiosks was farther away. As they reached them, and she opened her bag for some coppers, he reminded himself that in the half-light he could see that she had the shapeliest of lips, and that her nose was the least bit retroussé.

She found the coppers and turned to a box. She paused, turned back and for a moment, rested her hand on his arm.

'Thank you so much. I shall be all right now.'

The door closed behind her before he could say more than that he was delighted.

Mike and Thornton were waiting in the booking-hall and Mike was impatient. The blurred shapes of four policemen were also near by, and the body of the man who had been shot in the darkness was being loaded on to a stretcher.

11

The journey to Loftus's flat in the dark took longer than any of the trio wanted. The tiny lights of other traffic, the faint glow from shop-windows—little better even though regulations had been relaxed to some degree—and the road surfaces which glistened because of a faint drizzle of rain, helped to present London at its worst.

The cab slowed down.

'Here y'are, sir.' The driver reached backwards in the way London cabbies have, contorting himself rather than get out to open the door. The trio unloaded themselves on to the pavement outside 55g, Brook Street. Spats paid the man, and they went upstairs.

Once past the front door the lighting was better, and when a tall, very thin, and large-eyed young man opened the front door of the flat itself, the brilliance from within dazzled them for a moment. They stepped through into an atmosphere of smoke and fug and beer fumes, to meet another trio.

Sitting at ease in an easy-chair, yet telling the Errols that this meeting was important, was Gordon Craigie. That little-known man, who wielded such considerable but unsuspected influence in England, seemed a trifle thinner and a trifle greyer than when they had seen him a month before. His pale, lined face with the long, lantern jaw—a disgruntled jaw, some would say, despite the curved mouth with the humorous twist at the corners—seemed to have sunk a little at the cheeks, while his grey hair was thin and spread with some care on a cranium not wholly concealed. The sight of him had the same effect on Mark and Michael; they reproached themselves for complaining of fatigue, for Gordon Craigie's wide-set grey eyes seemed tired beyond words. They were the eyes of a man who could never catch up on sleep. Yet they were steady, and there was confidence in them.

A well-charred meerschaum, with a trail of tobacco

dangling from the bowl, drooped from his lips to his chest. He was dressed in grey, and his long, white hands were resting on the arms of the brown-leather chair. He nodded but did not smile as the Errols entered.

Bill Loftus was sitting opposite him.

Loftus was large and ungainly. That is, he looked ungainly because he created the impression that he was fat. Just why his tailor invariably failed to remove the impression of a too-large paunch no one knew, but it remained a fact. His shoulders were vast and tightly packed, and he had one of his massive legs over the arm of his chair. A fresh-complexioned face, topped with plentiful between-coloured hair, was not handsome. Yet it was pleasant to look upon, with the full lips, the sweeping jaw, and the large nose slightly out of true. His eyes, like Craigie's, were grey. Also, like Craigie's, they seemed to see far beyond the surface.

"Lo, folks,' said Bill Loftus, and he waved a hand towards a table on which reposed a small tankard. 'Have a spot?'

'Sit down,' said the tall, thin man who had opened the door. 'For this once I'll wait on you.'

Edward—Ned—Oundle, a friend of Loftus since earliest schooldays, was the antithesis of his mentor. They shared the flat and many other things in common, but there was nothing in common in their appearance. Though tall, Oundle was two inches shorter than Loftus, painfully thin, and ingenuous of countenance. This was chiefly due to his saucer-like blue eyes, so innocent and so appealing that many folk thought that he should be led gently from all contact with the evils of this world. His fair, crisp hair was like a halo above his round face, his cherub lips seemed sensitive, and there were times when his voice was soft and gentle.

Thus Craigie, Loftus and Oundle.

At that time they were the Big Three of Department Z,

Craigie the indisputable leader; Craigie had started the ultra-secret branch of British Intelligence, which he ran independently of the more widespread Espionage Branch. Loftus, his leading agent, was in many ways the best leader Craigie had had. Others had gone, either through death or marriage—the only things that could take a man from the service of the Department. Oundle was nominally Agent Number 2.

Thornton and the Errols were comparatively 'young' members.

The Errols had been with Craigie for less than a year, while Thornton had been transferred from the Espionage branch some eighteen months before.

Oundle brought beer, while the new-comers settled in easy-chairs, the Errols more leisurely than Thornton, who seemed ill at ease.

'Thanks,' said Mike, and drank. 'Not bad. Bill, in the first place a complaint—we didn't have time for any sleep.'

'Fair,' said Mark, quaffing also. 'In the second place, Bill, a complaint. There was nothing to it in the Sunny South.'

'In the third place...' began Mike.

'A complaint,' said Mark. 'You didn't warn us we were likely to be bumped off. Not friendly.'

Loftus rubbed his massive chin. 'Now all the fun and games are over,' he said, 'perhaps you'll dry up.' He glanced at Craigie, who nodded and thus gave permission for Loftus to talk for a while. 'There's some urgent stuff, Errols, you'll hear about it in due course. But just what happened at Waterloo?'

Thornton cleared his throat.

In the brighter light he seemed a positive Punch of a man, and he had regained his florid colour, which added to the illusion. Bright-blue eyes looked at Loftus steadily, as he lifted his hands palm upwards in a Gallic gesture.

'Sorry, Bill, but I don't see that I could have done anything at all. I met the Errols off the train, and this fellow...'

'What was he like?'

'Tallish—thinnish—swarthy,' said Thornton. 'I didn't see him in a good light, you'll have to go to the morgue for that. I did see that he had a round scar on his chin. He went up to the Errols and gave them a message which they thought was from you.'

Mike rubbed his cheek ruefully.

'We fell, too. Took it for granted when your name was mentioned that it was on the up-and-up.'

'It should learn you,' said Loftus, with a faint smile. 'What then?'

'They were going into a corner of the booking-hall,' said Spats, 'and I shone my torch for a moment. The man was going for his right pocket, and I assumed the worst. Mike hit him, and out fell the gun.'

'So it was to have been the worst,' said Mark.

'Ye-es,' said Loftus. 'And then?'

'Mike and I went off...' said Mark.

'For a drink,' completed Mike.

'And I stood by,' said Thornton. He looked puzzled and worried. 'No one came within three or four yards, I heard and saw nothing—but he was shot dead. The bullet took him through the temple.'

'Hmm,' said Loftus.

There was silence for some seconds, as if Loftus, Craigie and Oundle were deliberately digesting what they had heard.

'Well.' Craigie broke the silence, lifting his meerschaum out and probing at the bowl with a match, 'what do you make of it, Bill?'

'Thing is,' said Loftus, scratching his chin, 'the shot was fired from presumably four yards' distance. No one could see well enough at four yards to be sure of making a bull's-eye first shot—that's right, Spats?'

'Certainly,' agreed Thornton. 'It was the darkest corner of the hall—visibility about three yards.'

'And yet,' mused Loftus, 'one shot was enough. One shot and no noise. The lack of noise could be explained simply enough; an air-pistol was used, or one of these new silencers. But silent or not you can't shoot a man in the dark and be satisfied with one shot.'

'What puzzled me,' said Mike, 'is why he should go to that fuss and bother to get us to a dark spot when someone else could have put us away as easily as they did him.'

'A point,' said Loftus heavily, 'and in different circumstances an important one. It leaves open the question of whether the killed and the killer were working together, or apart. It offers the possibility that there are two parties concerned—one wanting to put you away, my Errols, and one which did put the would-be assassin away. But at the moment it's less important than the fact that death came in darkness.'

'Why?' asked Mike. 'No one else seems ready to fall for it.'

'Obviously,' said Loftus, 'the presumption is that the gunman knew what he was doing, and *could see* what he was doing. Spats saw nothing, which knocks out the possibility of a torch. So—how did the gunman see to kill?'

Mark stared. 'Gosh! You're suggesting...'

'He could *see* in the black-out,' gasped Mike.

'I am,' said Loftus, and Craigie cleared his throat, as if about to talk. 'It seems certain, and it's a thing to worry about. I'd like to be able to see by night these days, and here's someone who can.'

'Omitting,' said Oundle ingenuously, 'the possibility of a magnetic bullet...'

'Pipe down,' said Loftus. 'We've got the fact and we ought

to face it. Someone could see well enough in the dark to make sure of shooting straight. Apply the same principle to bombing straight, from the air. A something that gets over the black-out. Not a nice thought, but it's what we're up against. We've heard rumours before, but this is more than rumour. However, there are other things. Why did they pick on you...'

'And how they knew we were due,' said Mike.

'All in all,' said Loftus, 'we've plenty on our hands. Gordon will tell you that the Government's had word of another secret weapon, no less than this "see-in-the-dark" thing, and we've instructions to find it.'

'Germany...' began Thornton.

'As far as we know it's not in the hands of anyone in Berlin, Paris or London,' said Craigie, his dry voice with the barely noticeable Scottish accent following Thornton's without a pause. 'Either a neutral has it, or someone quite independent. It can cause havoc, and we've got to prevent it. I—what is it, Mark?'

For Mark Errol, at a moment when he should have been hanging on to his Chief's words, had exclaimed with some astonishment and was glancing down at his hand. Or what seemed to be his hand. Actually it was something along his sleeve, and he drew it out slowly, revealing a slip of pasteboard like a visiting-card with a pin in one end of it.

'Felt something sharp,' he said in a tone that was bewildered. 'This doesn't make sense.'

He stopped, and scowled, reading the words written on the card. Then he handed it to Craigie, and Loftus read it over his shoulder. It was brief and to the point:

Tell Craigie to keep out of this. If he doesn't it will only make things worse.

The others read it, and stared at Mark—who was remembering vividly the light touch of a girl's hand on his sleeve, and acknowledging that she could have pinned that card to his coat.

And he did not relish the thought.

3

WHO WAS THE LADY?

No,' said Loftus, and he replaced the telephone, 'there's no train for anywhere at 9.12, Mark. You fell completely.'

'I appear,' said Mark with some bitterness, 'to have fallen a lot since I reached England. She seemed...'

'Never mind what she seemed,' said Mike. 'Who was she?'

'I hadn't seen her in my life before,' said Mark, and then shrugged. 'No reason why I should have done, of course. I— good Lord, Gordon, have you realised that she saw *and* recognised me in the dark, or she wouldn't have pinned this card on? And the chap who's dead recognised us, which suggests he knew us well or saw us clearly.'

Craigie nodded soberly.

'I'd realised it, yes. They can see perfectly well in the dark.'

'It's fantastic,' said Mike.

'It's facts,' said Bill Loftus, and he grinned. 'I don't like fighting fantasy, but I don't mind a fracas with facts. Nice to look at, was she, Mark?'

'She was, and...'

He broke off, for Craigie stood up and stretched himself in front of the electric fire. He rubbed his hands in front of it for a moment, and looked like any family man about to retire for the night. Standing, he proved to be as tall as Oundle, and he looked round at the others while raising himself to and fro on his toes.

'We must face the situation as it is,' he said equably. 'In the first place, Mark, I wanted you and Mike quickly as there is an angle which you can handle. This little job was made for you. I didn't expect anyone would anticipate your arrival in England, and it seems reasonably obvious that whoever did the job knows that you are the only two available at the moment.'

'Hmm,' said Mike, 'it could explain something, yes.'

'We can take it for granted that you were watched at Southampton. Someone knew you had gone abroad and for all we know all the likely ports have been watched for you to come back. The message from the lady proves that your association with the Department is known, and also makes it obvious that they've assumed my interest in the puzzle.'

'In short, someone who knows us,' said Thornton.

'Too many people do,' admitted Craigie. 'We can't help that now. It could be an agent from any foreign country neutral or combatant, or a private individual. We know nothing except the rumour that a way of seeing through the dark has been invented,' admitted Craigie. 'Apart from that we start from scratch. We've since learned that someone is very anxious to stop us working on it. The someone might be (a) the inventor or (b) anyone who also wants to find the inventor.'

Oundle whistled.

'Which would explain our dago intending to kill, and the lads who actually killed him.'

'A point,' Mark grunted. 'But just what's on your mind for us, Gordon?'

Gordon Craigie pushed both hands deep in his pocket, and said:

'There is a man named Grafton, staying at a small hotel in Bournemouth. The Cliff Royal. An old man, who some months ago wrote to the Home Office and talked about seeing in the dark. The idea was investigated but turned down as impracticable. You'll find whether Grafton is still working on it, whether he has met any kind of trouble since getting in touch with the Home Office, and whether he's alone.'

Mike frowned. 'Or whether he's being watched.'

'That's it exactly,' said Craigie. 'Wally and Bob have been down there, but I had to take them off before they could do more than locate the hotel. The local police know nothing. You'll have time for a good rest, and to take the first train down in the morning.'

Mike pushed his hand through his hair.

'No other instructions?'

'All you can find about Grafton, that's all.'

'I'll wager,' said Mark gloomily, 'that he's an innocent, benevolent old gent who sleeps the clock round every night, and we will rusticate.' He drained his tankard, lifted a hand, and led the way towards the door.

The Errol family had not come out of the affair with honours, so far. It had the rudiments of excitement, though They talked little of it, however, while Pitcher—their man—had prepared everything they might need, and, as they walked up the stairs, was even running a bath. Pitcher was large and bulky, efficient but not obsequious, knowledgeable but not too curious. Pitcher was preparing a light meal before they went to bed, when the telephone rang. Mark was in the bath and Mike was struggling into pyjamas; Pitcher answered the telephone.

A low-pitched feminine voice said:

'Is that the home of Mr. Mark Errol?'

'Yes, ma'am.'

'Please tell Mr. Errol,' said the speaker, 'that he has already been advised what to do. That is all.'

'Things being as they are, and life being what it is,' said Spats Thornton, 'I'll clear off if there's nothing else at the moment.'

'You'll probably need plenty before this job's over,' said Loftus. 'Oh, and, Spats—don't let the job at the station worry you. It could have been me just as easily.'

'Or me,' admitted Craigie.

Spats left 55g, Brook Street much lighter-hearted than when he had entered it.

Craigie had told everyone virtually all he knew.

Talk of a ray with which anyone could see through darkness had percolated the mysterious channels of the Home Office, and reached the Cabinet. Craigie did not know how seriously the idea was considered by the Government, except that the Chief Lord had urged Wishart, the Prime Minister, to hand the investigation to Craigie. The First Lord, a man of push as well as ideas, was obviously impressed.

The only previous mention of such an invention had come from the old scientist, Matthew Grafton. Grafton was known as a man of fantastic ideas, and he was reputed to be a dreamer who rarely offered convincing evidence to support his discoveries.

This had reached Craigie the previous day, through Wishart. It was a bad time.

Department Z's best men were busy, many of them abroad. Rumours had come to them through different channels of secret weapons and other things. The terror had been let loose in Europe. Russia had revealed itself as an aggressor as naked as Germany.

It was no longer a question of trying to prevent war.

It was a matter of helping to make sure that the Allies won it.

Here, a little more than six months after the outbreak of war in which little had come up to expectations, when members of the public even admitted being bored, was the first whisper of something that *might* prove devastating.

Two major mysteries had presented themselves before Craigie's men had even started to operate.

'Which can't be avoided,' said Loftus, knocking out his pipe. 'I've a feeling things are going to happen soon, Gordon, and apparently we've two groups agin' us. Mark's lady friend intrigues me.'

Craigie tapped the mouthpiece of his pipe against strong white teeth.

'No one in their senses would expect to frighten us off.'

'Then why put us on our guard?' asked Oundle.

'They knew we were on to it,' said Loftus slowly. 'There's something deeper than we've seen yet, there was a definite object in the little lady's chat with Mark, and the killing of the would-be assassin. I'm going to see him. Coming, Gordon?'

'No, I'll go back to Whitehall. Don't come round unless you find anything out of the ordinary.'

'Right,' said Loftus. 'Hat and coat, Ned, for Gordon!'

Outside the flat two men were watching, junior agents of the Department. They followed Craigie's route, for they intended to take no chances of leaving the Chief without ample protection. One of them flashed a torch twice, for Loftus to see from the window where he was watching. He had turned out the light, but as he saw the torch he replaced the curtain, and Oundle switched on again.

'Ned, I don't like this a bit,' Loftus said.

'This being?'

'They *could* pick any one of us off in the same way.'

'Let us be cheerful,' said Oundle, and poured two tankards. 'Going alone?'

'No, you'd better come.'

They found a cab at a rank in Piccadilly, and were driven to Cannon Row, where the body of the man who had given the false message had been taken. The attendant at the morgue knew them, and they stepped into the dimly lighted underground building, in which the chill of death seemed to be on all sides. There were three shrouded figures on three stone tables, and the attendant took them to the one farthest from the door. A brighter light was switched on, and Loftus stared down at the swarthy, hollow-cheeked face of the man whom Mike had knocked out—and unwittingly sent to his last sleep.

'He's been photographed, sir, an' they took his prints. Mr. Miller's got them now.'

'Is he still at his office?' asked Loftus.

'Yes, sir.'

There was little about the face of the man to earn attention. In death the expression was peaceful enough, although even then there was a hungry look about him, as if he had been close to starvation. Loftus lifted back the shroud to see that the ribs and chest bones stuck through the stretched skin—and thus supported the evidence of the thin face.

He replaced the shroud, and the two agents went from Cannon Row to the Yard. The sergeant on duty in the main hall nodded as they went along to the large office which housed Superintendent Horace Miller. Miller—called, of course, Dusty—was a remarkable man in as much as he fitted his name to perfection. His sandy hair, sandy moustache, and pale skin always looked as if it were coated with a fine spray of flour. He might have stepped straight from a mill into the well-cut brown suit which clad his heavy body when Loftus and Oundle went in. He was sitting at a large desk near the window; there was one other desk, empty at the moment, and occupied usually by Chief Inspector Frazer, Miller's aide.

Miller was the liaison officer between the Yard and Department Z. All work which Loftus and the others handled, needing police attention, went through Miller—unless Sir William Fellowes, the Assistant Commissioner, handled it himself. Miller was a forthright officer, lacking a little in imagination who frequently confessed himself appalled by the risks which Loftus took. There had been a time when Miller had been unable to understand the apparent casualness of Craigie's men, but he had come to realise that their manner was a natural result of the strain in which they worked, to understand that if they laughed or made a quip in the presence of death it was not through callousness.

Miller stood up as they went in.

'Evening,' he said heavily, 'I've been expecting you. How are things?'

'Bad,' answered Loftus.

'I'm not surprised.' Miller stopped smiling, and touched a small heap of oddments on his desk. Next to the heap was a manilla folder, and he opened it. 'We haven't found much, I'm afraid.'

'Huh,' said Loftus, an expression which he favoured—the result, Oundle claimed, of his devotion to tales of the rip-roaring Wild West. 'No name, no address, no records?'

'No,' said Miller. 'A few oddments—we might trace him, for there's a penknife that looks new, and a cheap watch he can't have had more than a week or two—the case isn't scratched worth speaking of. For the rest...'

He pushed the pile over to Loftus, who examined the

penknife, the cheap nickel watch, a few coppers, two half-crowns, a piece of string and—something he turned over twice—a worn piece of billiards chalk. The small round box in which the chalk had been wrapped was missing, and a segment had been chipped out of the block itself.

'Thought of this, Horace?'

'Yes,' said Miller, 'but there's not much chance of locating him through that. I'll try, though. Ah—that's the only thing that puzzles me.'

'That' was a small round disc, a little larger than a ha'-penny. It was plain on one side, made of copper, and well worn at the edges. Loftus flicked it into the air, and it gave forth a light *ting* as his thumb-nail struck it. Oundle peered at it with him, seeing the design on the one side.

The design was nearly worn off, but with the help of a magnifying-glass which Miller took from his pocket, Loftus could make out what looked like two heads on one pair of shoulders. He grinned crookedly.

'Accident or design, I wonder?'

'Of course it's a design,' said Miller.

'Come, come,' said Loftus, 'I mean accident or design that the dead man had it on him. You'll keep the fingerprints and whatnot filed, won't you? And you might try the other countries, to see if he's on the records there.'

'It's being done,' said Miller, stroking his moustache.

'Quick work from Scotland Yard,' said Loftus. 'Mind if I keep this?' He tucked the disc into his pocket, and Miller smiled dourly.

'A lot of use it would be if I'd said no,' he commented. 'What is it all about, Loftus?'

'I wish I knew,' said Loftus. 'But you'll be in on it as soon as anyone. How's crime in the black-out?'

'It could be worse,' said Miller cautiously.

In the courtyard of Police Headquarters Loftus stopped, as if hesitating while deciding whether to go into Parliament Street or to the Embankment. It was a pitch-black night, and there was little traffic about. Loftus kept quite still, and Oundle followed his example. Oundle had learned many years before that Loftus did nothing without a reason.

Loftus gripped his arm, and whispered.

'There's someone not four yards from us, Ned.'

'Probably a policeman.'

'And possibly not. Move towards the left, and ask me whether it's worth going back to the Yard for some matches.'

Oundle obeyed, without question. He moved slowly, and with his ears strained and his eyes at a stretch to try to pierce the gloom. As he said 'matches' he heard a sharp exclamation, followed by Loftus's:

'I'm awfully sorry! No damage, I hope?'

'N-no.' Whoever he had hit against had been startled, and Oundle grinned. Loftus caught up with him, after another hearty apology, and they walked briskly into Parliament Street. There were taxis in the middle of the road, but Loftus preferred to walk, keeping a sharp pace and cannoning into several people. Deliberately he did not use a torch. As deliberately he took three side turnings on the way to Piccadilly. It took them twenty minutes to reach 55g, Brook Street, and outside the house Loftus took his torch out for the first time.

'I'm not sure on my own doorstep,' he said aloud, 'but I knew the rest like the palm of my hand. Ah!'

The bright beam of his torch shot out, but did not point towards the door. Instead, it revealed a short, thick-set man who stood no more than three yards away from them. It revealed his face, a florid, startled countenance, chiefly remarkable at that moment because the mouth was open, and a tooth was missing from the upper jaw.

'Sorry!' said Loftus heartily.

He swivelled the torch round, but not until he had shone it on the stranger's coat—where, Oundle glimpsed, there was a pale mark. Oundle frowned, but not until they were in the flat did Loftus say gently:

'He followed us from the Yard. He was on our heels all the way but we didn't hear him, which meant he had some yards to spare.'

'Sure it's the same man?'

'Quite sure,' said Loftus casually, 'I rubbed the billiards chalk on his coat. Odd thing, my Ned.'

'Meaning he could see us?'

'It looks as if he could,' admitted Bill Loftus, and he too sounded sombre. 'And if he could it's the very Devil. I...'

He broke off, and moved like lightning for the door. Oundle was on his heels, and as Loftus pulled the door open the scream which had made him move came more loudly into the flat—a scream that was coming from the street, nearby.

4

OUT OF THE DARKNESS

They had heard it clearly because the window was open behind the curtain, and the room faced the street. Neither of them had hesitated, despite the gloom, but Loftus's torch carved a ray of light towards the pavement as soon as he opened the front door. The scream had stopped, but there was a low-pitched, moaning sound in its stead—and the thought that sprung into both their minds was proved to be justified.

A man was lying on the pavement, opposite the house.

There were footfalls coming from each end of Brook Street, and several torches flashed. No one was as near as Loftus, however, and he was on his knees peering into the man's face before anyone else. Oundle saw that in the extremity of pain the man's mouth was open.

And he saw the gap in the upper row of teeth.

'Our man,' he said, and he spoke almost casually.

'How?'

'Shot,' said Loftus. 'Not quite such a good aim, it got him in the neck, poor beggar. I—ah, officer, I've been expecting you.'

He stood up as a policeman arrived, with two men close behind. 'I heard the scream from my flat, and hurried down.'

'*So* I gathered, sir,' said the policeman heavily. 'I—oh, it's Mr. Loftus.' That it was Loftus seemed to put everything right with the world, and the policeman in uniform bent down to investigate the man lying on the pavement but no longer moaning. He was dead—dead in the opinion of the policeman, Loftus, the two strangers who had arrived, and a doctor summoned from a nearby house.

To Loftus and to Oundle there was something worse than death in that fact.

How had he been shot?

Who had killed him?

And why had he been killed?

'The why,' said Loftus into the telephone to Craigie, 'being the most important, Gordon. It seems senseless. Two men who followed us—or some of us—put out apparently just because of that. There's neither rhyme nor reason to it.'

'There is, and we'll find what it is,' said Craigie, who did not sound tired over the telephone. 'I've heard from Mark Errol—that girl telephoned him and repeated the warning.'

'Did she, by Jove! Infernal impudence. Gordon, could this killing be aimed at making us go warily? Putting the wind up us.'

'It's even likely to be, Bill. Who has the second man?'

'I've sent him to Cannon Row.'

'I'll phone Miller so that he looks into it personally,' said Craigie. 'We'll want the bullets compared, they may have come from the same gun. No luck with identifying the first man?'

'Only that he plays billiards.'

'It might help,' said Craigie. 'All right, get some sleep while you can.'

Yet Loftus did not go to bed particularly early, although

Oundle was asleep soon after eleven. Loftus sat smoking in an easy-chair, the smoke from his pipe coiling upwards towards the haze in the ceiling, and the air in the room getting thicker every minute. He was trying to make sense out of nonsense, trying to see reason in insanity.

'Ta-ra-ri-a-tida,' carolled Mike Errol, 'ta-ra-ri-a-tidy.' He stopped, and said to the bathroom: 'That's if nobody minds me saying so.'

He rubbed down quickly and, with the sun streaming through the windows of the passage beyond, walked briskly to the bedroom which he was sharing with his cousin. It was his first morning in Bournemouth, and he was liking it. The sun gleamed on the yellow sands at the foot of the cliffs which he could see from the windows, and there was a blue haze about the water, while a small sailing-ship ploughed its way steadily towards Swanage, its sail picked out clear and white. Two or three smaller boats were bobbing on the swell close to the shore, and the buildings of the West Cliff, mostly with red roofs glistening in the sun, made it look like a toy town. The pines, tops driven backwards from the sea, added a touch of dark green which set the rest into perfect relief.

The previous day had been one of complete inactivity and rest. Much rest: and both Mike and Mark decided that as Loftus had sent them on a dead-end job again they may as well make the most of it.

Matthew Grafton *was* at the Cliff Royal. They had actually argued with him on the previous evening, debating the respective merits of the British and Nazi air forces. The scientist considered that the Nazis were underrated, and the British much overrated. The Errols had begged leave to disagree.

31

The hotel was on the cliff-edge, some ten minutes' walk from the pier, and comfortably away from traffic and noise. A little backwater for the Errols, and a place of comfort after their experiences of small French estaminets, and tiny Italian inns. There was ample hot water, central heating, spring-interior mattresses, and excellent food. It was Mike's morning for breakfast.

There being no apparent need for them both to be on the prowl all the time, Mark was to laze as he liked that morning, Mike the next day. The possibility of a sudden recall had been borne in mind, and they had chosen to ignore it.

Mike opened the bedroom door, to find Mark had sent for more tea, and was reading the *Daily Telegraph*.

'News?' asked Mike.

'Someone's dropped another leaflet somewhere,' said Mark.

'Nice work. Any more secret weapons?'

'Don't talk to me about secret weapons,' said Mark with a scowl. 'She pinned one on to my sleeve. Someone's protesting to Berlin about the sinking of a freighter.'

'What are the apologies on, silver or gold salvers?'

'Your trouble,' said Mark, 'is an inability to take anything as seriously as you should. Get some clothes on, the gong'll go at any minute, and you'll want to make sure the Professor's grape-fruit isn't poisoned.' He tossed the paper aside, and Mark began to dress.

'Everything considered, Mike, there's a lot of funny business about this. In the circumstances Gordon wouldn't have sent us down here just for fun and games.'

'No-o. He's expecting developments with the Professor.'

'Who said he was a professor, anyway?'

'The large woman with the Spanish comb behind her ear,'

said Mark. 'The one who said Freud was to blame for the attack on Poland.'

'With the voice that breathed o'er Eden,' admitted Mike, stooping to tie his shoe-laces. 'Large fore and aft, and very earnest. An eagle eye on the Professor, who has to be careful or he'll be hauled into matrimony.'

'You seem,' said Mark, 'to have noticed her. Nice soul. I'll wage a pound to a penny that she gets into the breakfast-room a minute after the Pro—I mean Grafton—and neither more nor less. I—hurry!'

Mike hurried, for the breakfast gong went.

There was no real reason why he should be in the breakfast-room before Grafton, but they had decided to do their job seriously and to the best of their ability see that Grafton was kept in sight most of the day. Mike finished knotting his tie, and went downstairs. Sun, which had been missing most of that spring, was still shining through the windows, and in his ears as he passed an open door leading to a small garden was the lapping of the waves against the seashore. A maid, pert and neat in cap and apron, was the only occupant of the breakfast-room.

The Professor's table was in a corner by the window, and reasonably close to the bright coal fire. The Errols had chosen a table from which they could see their quarry without turning their heads. There were fifteen tables in all, eight set for four, and seven for two—although at dinner the previous night only seven had been occupied, Mike and Mark making the only double. They were opposite the door, and it opened to reveal—Mike anticipated—one of the dowdy females who had been in the previous night.

The woman who entered was medium tall, inclined to be willowy, fair-haired, and very English. Also very lovely. She had one of those dream complexions which seemed to owe nothing to make-up, but actually owed a great deal, if discreetly. Her eyes were blue, clear, and starry. Her lips were red but not too red, an inclination of her head as she passed Mike was a thing of grace.

'I don't,' said Mike to his grape-fruit, 'believe it.'

She was dressed in a suit coat and a white blouse which somehow contrived to make her look incredibly tiny and dainty. She carried a *Daily Telegraph* and when she greeted the maid in attendance her voice was pleasant without being affected.

And then she sat at the Professor's table.

'I don't believe that either,' said Mike, and he finished his appetiser without enjoyment. It was all wrong. He should have had some kind of warning, and...

'Good morning, darling!'

A male voice, deep and full of the joy of living, a painful thing to hear so early. Mike heard it before seeing the door open, for he had been too busy looking at the girl. Now he saw a man of some thirty years, reasonably tall, passably good-looking, and with a positive rock of a chin, enter the breakfast-room and without fuss or bother sit opposite the girl. That was annoying for two reasons. It meant that he was at her table, and that Mike could not see her without craning his neck.

'Hallo, Teddy,' said the girl amiably.

'Teddy!' thought Mike Errol with a snort. 'Teddy! Nothing more than a bruiser, he...' Mike stopped thinking and ordered bacon and eggs—hoping that the rationing would make it permissible and gave himself time to smile at himself. There was, after all, nothing unusual nor abnormal about a decent-looking man and a good-looking girl greeting each other at the breakfast table as if they were old friends. Bias apart, moreover the man was a clean-cut fellow with a naturally deep voice.

The puzzle was the table.

Why should they go to the Professor's?

Others filtered into the breakfast; a chorus of 'good mornings' and a combined rustling of newspapers followed. The only conversation came from the corner by the window, and that was not well maintained. Mike saw the girl glancing towards the door several times, and once as she turned her head the man leaned forward and whispered.

The girl shrugged.

Within a minute her eyes had turned towards the door again, and a movement of her companion revealed her clearly to Mike. He scowled, for he thought at once that she looked worried— and he did not like to think of her worried. He had come to the conclusion that she was a relative or friend of Grafton's.

If he were right, she was looking for Grafton. Of her growing concern there could not be the slightest doubt. He saw her push her plate away suddenly, with her food half-finished.

'I'll slip up to make sure he's all right,' she said.

'I'll go,' said the man cheerfully. 'But there's nothing to worry about.'

He suited his action to his words, dabbed at his lips with his napkin. Mike found himself watching the door as eagerly as the girl.

The rustling increased, the clatter of knives and forks went on, but the door did not open. It passed through Mike's mind that the well-built woman who had blamed Freud for so many things had not yet arrived, and he recalled Mark's offer to wager that she would follow the Professor by a minute.

He had finished eating and was deliberately dallying in

order to watch the girl. Now he pushed his chair back and walked towards the door. Attractive though she was, his interest was in Grafton, and her anxiety could only be for the Professor.

A maid entered the room hurriedly and stepped across to the girl.

'Mr. Grey would like to see you for a minute, miss.'

Mike was outside the room before the girl had left the table. Presumably 'Mr. Grey' was the man who had left earlier, and his message suggested some reason for the girl's anxiety.

Grafton's room was Number 11. The Errols had Number 15, which was on the same landing, and as Mike reached the landing he saw that the door of Number 11 was wide open. Passing it, he glimpsed Grey standing by the window with his back towards the door.

The girl was hurrying in Mike's wake.

Mike went quickly into his own room, where Mark, in his dressing-gown, was breakfasting by the open window. His expression hardened as he saw his cousin.

'Get some clothes on,' said Mike, 'we may have a hurried move.'

He waited for nothing else but ducked back into the passage. The Professor's door remained open, and the girl's voice was coming quietly. The quiet note was praiseworthy in the circumstances.

'He can't have gone far, Teddy.'

'Of course not.' The voice of the man was hearty, and obviously intended to be reassuring. To Mike, it failed in its object. 'He's slipped out for a stroll along the cliff, it's such a glorious morning.'

'Don't try to tell me what he's likely to do, please.' For the first time there was a note of impatience in the girl's voice, suggesting that she was a little tired of Teddy's heartiness.

Mike silently applauded her. 'I—I'm sorry, Teddy, but you know that it's been so worrying for the past few weeks, and I've been afraid of something like this for a long time.'

'Easy goes,' said Teddy. 'We'll take a stroll, and probably run across him. I know he's going to be my father-in-law, sweet, but he *is* unpredictable.'

'Ye-es.' Mike could imagine the expression on her face, and at the same time digested the fact that she was Grafton's daughter and that Teddy was engaged to her: presumably, that was. She went on, in a quiet voice that took Mike completely by surprise. 'Teddy, did you see those two men last night?'

'Which two?'

'The young ones. They were in the lounge when we walked through, and one of them was in the breakfast-room this morning. Who are they?'

'Good Lord!' exclaimed Teddy. 'Probably a couple of clerks on holiday. Don't start getting ideas about strangers, Jan.'

'If they were clerks, I'm a typist,' said the girl, so downrightly that Mike came out of his momentary surprise, and felt even grateful. 'They're the last type to come to a hotel like this for a holiday on their own. Teddy—will you go and ask them whether they've seen Dad?'

'Eh?' Teddy seemed startled.

'Oh, I'll go,' said the girl impatiently. 'You'd probably notice nothing, even if he was under their bed!'

Mike retreated hastily, combining a surprised satisfaction at her idea, and amusement at her attitude towards Teddy. She seemed to hold Teddy in a kind of tolerant contempt, and certainly she had no great opinion of him. Odd, for a fiancée. Mike forgot that oddness as he reached the room, to find Mark dressed and about to leave the dressing-table. He slipped in, closed the door quietly, and sat hastily in an easy-chair.

'Visitors,' he said. 'Someone's throwing something into our laps. Professor's missing, or daughter thinks he is. Boy-friend sceptical. Be prepared for...'

He did not complete the sentence, for he heard hurried footsteps along the passage and a moment later there was a tap at the door. He said 'come in', casually, and when he saw her he jerked up from his chair in surprise. Mark, a brush in his hand, held it a few inches from his hair, and stared.

'*Good* morning,' said Mike, and his smile was beatific.

She spoke quietly. 'This is going to sound absurd, I'm afraid, but have either of you been out this morning?'

She had entered the room and closed the door behind her, and she was watching Mark and Mike closely.

'I'm afraid not. Lazing and all that,' Mike said. 'Mark even had breakfast in the room, but he's notoriously bad in the mornings. Dare I ask why?'

'My father went out, I think, and I wanted to know which way he went.'

'Father?' asked Mike hopefully.

'Mr. Grafton...'

'I'm afraid I'm rather at a loss,' admitted Mike. 'Names on the first day at these places are a bit difficult, you know. If you care to describe him it might help.'

'It can't if you haven't been out,' said the girl. Mike could almost see her wishing that she had not come—and for some absurd reason imagined Teddy reminding her that he had been against it from the first. 'He's old, and white-haired...'

'Oh, the Professor!' exclaimed Mark from the dressing-table. 'We were having a fierce argument in the lounge last night. No, I haven't seen him.'

'But we'll know him like a shot and we'll gladly have a look round,' volunteered Mike. 'One go one way, the other t'other. Don't say "no", we're on holiday, and there's nothing to do.

Mark needs the exercise, anyhow. By the way, our name is Errol. Cousins, not twins. Mark and Mike, to our friends.'

He looked his question.

'Janice Grafton,' she said, and she gave the impression that she was not thinking of what she was saying. 'It's good of you, but...'

'It's gone, it's gone! They've stolen it!'

The words came from the passage, high-pitched, angry, and in a man's voice. A voice all three recognised, for it was the Professor's. Mike moved quickly towards the door, but the girl reached it first, and flung it open. They were in time to see the old man, with his white hair awry and his coat-tails flying behind him, disappearing into Room 11, and shouting:

'It's gone, I tell you! Disappeared completely! They've stolen it!'

5

THE PROFESSOR'S PAPERS

J anice Grafton hurried after her father, while the Errols
followed fast, determined not to lose this chance. As
Mark reached Mike he whispered:

'They're all batty, the girl as well.'

'You leave that girl alone.'

'Beauty leaves me cold, after Wednesday night,' murmured
Mark. 'She's probably Hitler's loveliest spy.' He grinned
crookedly as they entered Number 11 without asking permission—but with excuse, for the girl had left the door open.

Grafton was standing with his back to the window, his
hands lifted to the level of his head, horn-rimmed glasses
fallen a little down his nose. He looked wild, even fanatical, for
his bright-blue eyes were prominent, and a shock of white
hair was standing up on end. His face was lean and impressive.
A long nose, bushy eyebrows, thin but unusually long lips, and
a pointed jaw all held character. His skin was pale, but it
looked hard and weatherbeaten, resembling old parchment.
Above a butterfly collar and a flowing, untidy bow was a
prominent Adam's apple, making the scraggy neck look even

more ancient. The rest of him was thin, clad in old-fashioned morning clothes. His shaking hands were knuckly and rheumy at the joints.

'Teddy' was sitting on the foot of the bed.

A 'nice' young man, thought Mike, but somewhat vacuous. He would be good form in everything but probably lacked a single idea of his own.

The drawers of the dressing-table and the tallboy had been emptied, and most of their contents were strewn on the floor. The wardrobe door was open, and a few oddments lay at the foot of it.

The Errols took it all in at a glance, and while Grafton was shouting:

'The moment I woke up I knew that someone had been in the room, curse them! *Blast* them! The thieving, murdering scoundrels, coming into my room, stealing—stealing!—my papers! Two years' work—two years' work gone!'

Mark was watching the girl—and he saw her looking at the old man with a queer expression in her eyes. It was as if she was seeing something she could not believe.

And she was looking at her own father.

'Daddy, please be quiet.' She spoke incisively, but with a considerable effort. 'You'll probably find them later in the morning. Where have you been?'

'To look for them, where else do you think?' shouted Grafton. 'I can't spend all my time in bed like you lazy young hussies of today. Someone came in here while I was asleep, and the papers were stolen! You know what that means. You know, don't you?'

'Yes, of course,' said Jan Grafton soothingly. 'But it may not prove as bad as you think, perhaps they've been mislaid.' Despite her words, both Mark and Michael saw that she was speaking under considerable strain—as if she saw something which frightened her. The only likely thing was her concern at the loss of the papers. 'Have you had breakfast yet?'

'Breakfast!' screeched the Professor. 'The most important papers of my life, and she talks about breakfast! Paugh! Get out—get out with this—this playboy you're going to marry, go and...'

Quite suddenly and without warning, he collapsed.

He seemed to crumple, bending from the knees first, and then falling, not heavily, to the carpet. The girl jumped forward, and Teddy sprang from the bed. Quickly though they moved, however, Mike Errol reached that weedy frame first. He had a swift mental picture of a man with a small hole in his temple—and this man had collapsed as if he had been shot.

Grafton had not.

His pulse was beating, although unevenly. He was breathing, and as the seconds passed and without speaking Mike lifted him to the bed, it grew stertorous. Mark spoke quietly.

'Does he do this often, do you know?'

'Ye-es.' Janice was staring at her father with a mingling of fear and horror in her eyes. The whole atmosphere was strange and strained—and unreal. The old man's outburst and then his collapse had been theatrical in themselves. The girl's manner increased the theatricality, while 'Teddy' stood by, hands deep in his pockets and looking far more annoyed than worried. 'Playboy' suited him. Nothing else rang true.

'Will he need a doctor?' Mark demanded, a little testily.

'No, I'll get a powder.' Janice Grafton turned to the dressing-table and began to rummage through a drawer which was already pulled out. Some of the contents were on the floor, but she brought forth a small white box, and took from it a powder in a folded slip of paper. While the three men stood by she mixed it with water and then poured it into Grafton's mouth, Mike and Mark supporting the unconscious man as she did so.

'Thank you.' She put the glass down, and stood staring at Grafton. 'I think he'll be all right now.'

'What about the papers?' asked Mike promptly. 'If they've been lost we may be able to find 'em.'

Janice pushed a hand across her forehead, and then over her hair, smoothing it straight back. She stepped to the window and sat down, while Teddy Grey watched her anxiously. In a low voice, empty of all expression, the girl said:

'Don't worry about it, please. Father is—a little eccentric. There were no papers.'

'What?' exclaimed Mark.

'My dear Jan!' began Grey. 'I...'

He stopped abruptly as she looked across at him, and Mike interrupted the look. She thanked him again, shook hands, but did not go with the Errols to the door. Nor did Grey.

Outside Mike cocked his head on one side.

'Batty,' said Mark. 'I'm not surprised, he looked that way.'

'Who's batty?' demanded Mike.

'Grafton, obviously.'

'I thought you'd seen yourself as others see you,' said Mike acidly. He turned into Number 11, and sat on the bed, leaning back with his hands linked behind his neck. Mark, not well pleased, glared down at him.

'Mr. Grey,' said Mike dreamily, 'was as surprised as you and me that there were no papers, and he should know a little about it. The Professor cracked up because some papers, he thought, were stolen. The girl says there are no papers, but I've a feeling she lied, which is a pity with a pretty girl. However—one of us had better phone Bill or Craigie from a call-box. The other ought to keep an eye on the girl, and we must have a third down here. Grey wants watching.'

'I'll slip out and phone Bill,' Mark said.

Mike waited on the bed, leaving the door ajar and listening keenly although most of the time he appeared to be asleep. For ten minutes there was no sound from Room 15, but a door opened and closed sharply, and footsteps sounded. He reached the door in time to see Janice Grafton and her fiancé walking down the stairs.

Grey sounded peeved.

'Hang it, old girl, there's no sense in getting yourself worked up like this about it. He'll be as right as rain, and there's no reason why we shouldn't have a walk together.'

She stopped and turned abruptly, and her voice had an edge to it.

'Teddy, are you going to be obstinate or are you going to *try* to be helpful? One of us must stay here until he comes round, and I need a walk.'

'Oh—all right.' Grey seemed reluctant. 'If it's like that I suppose I'd better stay. I suppose,' he added sarcastically, 'it will be all right if I stay in the lounge?'

'Quite all right,' said Janice, tensely.

'All,' thought Mike, 'is certainly not right in that dovecote.'

He made his way down the stairs, reaching the front door a few seconds after the girl had gone out and Grey had entered the lounge. The door led to Ervin Drive, a wide thoroughfare with trees and shrubs lining it. A pleasant spot, if not an exciting one. Other small hotels were on either side, and the kerbs and trees—the latter to a height of three or four feet— were painted white, more evidence of the efforts to prevent accidents in the black-out.

The thought sobered Mike Errol.

He saw Janice Grafton some thirty yards away. She had turned right, and was walking towards a road leading to the sea. The shrubs and trees were helpful, for they made it difficult for her to see him, even if she turned her head.

She hesitated for a moment in the road which ran along the cliff, and then turned right, away from Bournemouth and going towards the Sandbanks direction. There were few people about, and most of those who were, walked slowly— the older residents of a town which at times seemed to comprise of nothing but old people. A Pekinese snapped at Janice's ankles, but she walked on oblivious to it, while the owner called her Fido back in mock reprimand.

There was a quiet wind blowing from the sea, and the tide was in, lapping against the sands beneath and yet seeming to add to the quiet. From the distance came the only discordant note now that the dog had stopped—a motor-horn sounded stridently. The sharp tapping of the girl's heels on the road surface came, too—Mike's approach was barely audible, for he wore rubber heels.

Janice's height had grace with it, and her fair hair was blowing backwards, catching the rays of the sun as they shone across the sea. She walked easily and very erect.

A car came from behind Mike and began to slow down as it approached Janice. There were trees and rough land on either side of the road at that spot, and no apparent need for a car to stop. Mike had glimpsed the driver, but all he could remember of him was that he was a youngish man. The car was a Morris ten or twelve, dark blue, and nearly new.

The car stopped alongside the girl.

Mike could just see the top of her head as she turned. He did not need cover, but he stepped behind a tree so that he should not be noticed if she moved. He could hear voices, but caught no words.

'Queerer,' quoth Mike to the trees about him, 'and queerer.

I wonder if our johnnies can invent something to hear at a distance too.'

The driver of the Morris had stepped out, and he walked with the girl some yards farther from Mike. Mike had made a mental note of the car's number, and was prepared to wait there for ten minutes or more when he heard the high-powered whine of a powerful engine climbing a steep gradient. There was such a gradient behind him. He turned, more from curiosity than anything else, to see a Bugatti with two passengers, as well as a driver, reach and pass him.

And he saw something in one passenger's hand.

It happened as quickly as that—a gun. Mike moved his right hand to his pocket swiftly, shouting:

'Look out, there!'

The Bugatti slowed down, and one of the passengers was on his feet. He made a silhouette against the sea, gun raised and pointing towards the couple.

He fired.

Mike did also, almost simultaneously. He heard a shout of pain, and saw the man stagger, the gun falling from his grasp. He saw the other passenger, a man with a remarkably long and pale face turned towards him—and the driver trod more heavily on the accelerator, the Bugatti gathered speed again.

'Not,' said Mike aloud, 'if I know it.'

He squeezed the trigger. A stream of bullets spat out, short stabs of flame with them, the muffled snorts of the silenced automatic the only sounds. He aimed low deliberately, for the Bugatti's near-side tyre, and he saw the big car swerve; a fraction of a second later he heard the loud report of a bursting tyre.

Mike's gun was empty, and he started to move but thought better of it, for the Bugatti was reeling across the road towards the edge of the cliffs, and the lean-faced man was firing towards him, bullets hummed like wasps about his ears. A bullet struck the trunk of a tree. He caught a glimpse of Paleface jumping from the Bugatti, he was in time to see the big car strike against a tree, sheer off towards the left, and then sway sideways. It had crashed through the frail wooden fencing that kept the narrow strip of rough land from the roadway—a strip bordered on the far side by the sheer cliff edge.

The driver leapt but as he went his coat caught in the steering-wheel, and he sprawled downwards, neither out of the Bugatti nor in it. The car disappeared, dropping abruptly out of sight.

'God!' gasped Mike.

Nearly a hundred yards ahead of him the man with the pale face was moving fast, the only one of the trio from the Bugatti likely to escape with his life. Mike began to run, passing Janice and the obviously wounded man at speed, intent only on reaching his quarry. Paleface stopped abruptly and quite coolly. Mike was going fast, and could see everything clearly, vividly, and yet was unable to do anything to help himself. It was an odd moment, and in it he had a queer impression of the man from the Bugatti; it was as if he *felt* the other's complete self-control, as if he *knew* that nothing would ever harass or perturb the man.

The other held a gun.

It was either a second gun or the original one which he had reloaded while running. He took aim swiftly and fired three times. The first two bullets missed. The third stabbed through Mike's thigh, and he pitched forward, partly from pain, partly from impact. He fell shoulder-first, a last-moment turn saving his head from striking the road.

Breathless, and unable to move, he saw his man running effortlessly towards the first turning right. Only then—so swiftly had things happened—did he hear the resounding crash. He knew what had happened the moment he heard it, and he screwed his neck round, looking towards the spot where the Bugatti had gone over the cliff. There was a moment's pause and then he saw dust rising—or smoke, he could not be sure which.

He tried to get up, but failed.

He began to crawl towards the edge of the cliff, going beneath the guard rail. But he had not gone ten feet before he heard the whine of a car engine again, and knew that another powerful car was coming up the hill. He looked towards it, and he saw a black Talbot as it pulled up with a squealing of brakes alongside the Morris.

And he wondered whether Pale-face had contrived to return.

Instead Loftus and Oundle stepped out.

Far below—it seemed a mile, but was little more than six hundred feet—Loftus and Oundle saw what was left of the Bugatti. It was in flames, which were keeping a dozen men and women at bay. Pieces of debris littered the promenade below.

They saw one other thing.

Near the car was the body of a man, spread out at a peculiar angle, ugly and horrible even at that distance. The face was turned upwards, clear in the sun—the face of a dead man.

Loftus allowed himself only a moment to see all this, then knelt down by Mike's side.

'Now let's have a look at you,' he said. 'Where did you get what?'

'A piece of lead,' said Mike, 'in the thigh. Unless it's my imagination.'

Loftus located the small hole in the trousers, and without ado took a razor-keen knife from his pocket and cut a piece out large enough for him to see the blood-soaked cotton trunks which Mike was wearing. He cut the leg of them, and saw the wound—well on the outside of the thigh, bleeding freely, and yet not serious.

'Another quarter of an inch and it would have missed you,' he said. 'We won't need an ambulance, anyhow. What are the people like at your hotel?'

'All right. Why?'

'You'll be an invalid for a few days, I think,' opined Loftus, cleaning the wound with his handkerchief. 'We'd better find a nursing-home for you, and one where they won't ask a lot of unnecessary questions.'

'But dammit...'

'Uncle Bill has spoken,' said Loftus firmly, and there would be no arguing. 'Let me give you a hand.'

Even Mike was startled by the ease with which the big man lifted and carried him towards the Talbot.

By that time Janice Grafton was sitting in the Morris, and the man she had met was on his feet. He had a head wound, which bled slightly, and Oundle was helping him into the smaller car.

Janice Grafton was staring straight ahead of her—and Mike was reminded of her expression when she had looked at her father after his collapse.

6
JEREMIAH WARNCLIFFE

S itting in a large room at Whitehall, Gordon Craigie lifted one of the five telephones on his desk and, without a change of expression, listened to a deep voice spelling:

'S-U-T-F-O-L.'

'All right, Bill,' said Craigie.

It was a simple code, and one which had never leaked out from the Department itself. To make sure that a caller was genuine the agent spelt his name backwards.

Craigie worked everything out with equal care. Which is not to suggest that the Department men never made mistakes; the very exigencies and tempo of their work made errors inevitable. Craigie considered his most important task that of sifting of mistakes that mattered from those which were of no importance. No agent was blamed for a mistake; those few who made too many disappeared from the Department's active list.

The affair of the invention which it was reckoned could nullify the effect of the black-out was likely to be far-reaching. Craigie and Loftus had seen the possible ramifications far more quickly than the other agents. Both men had been chary of accepting the rumour as true, but the two deaths which had occurred offered convincing truth. At first, the Grafton angle had seemed a possible source of information, although the Errols had been sent down—as Mike had shrewdly suspected—to combine a watching brief with a rest.

And then, with the suddenness so frequently affecting the activities of the Department, word had come from Craigie's resident agent in the small neutral country of Vania. Vania was neither a Baltic State nor one of the Scandinavian countries, but held a position of critical importance between the two. It was virtually an island, although actually a peninsular connected with the Danish mainland by a long, narrow strip of land strongly reinforced on either side, and with a road and railway running its full length. It was the obvious starting point of German hostilities against the Scandinavian countries and the miracle was that the Vanian monarchist Government had contrived so far to maintain the balance between the warring Powers of democracy and dictatorship.

Like Holland, Belgium, and the larger Scandinavian countries, Vania had become a clearing-house for propaganda, news, unobtainable from other sources and—because of its position—the north European headquarters of the secret services of the bigger Powers.

From Craigie's leading resident agent, had come word of the new invention which would counteract the usefulness of darkness, which brought to a head the efforts of countless scientists to invent an apparatus by which it was possible to see without light.

Berlin had heard of the discovery, and wanted it.

Berlin had sent agents to England, and the name of Matthew Grafton had been mentioned.

Grafton was considered by Berlin to be the key man...

On hearing this, Craigie had sent Loftus and Oundle post haste to Bournemouth, and now Loftus was on the telephone, with Craigie waiting in his large, untidy office of news.

'Let me give you the basic story first,' Loftus said, and passed on with brevity and remarkable lucidity everything he had learned from Mike Errol. Then he went on: 'I don't know what to make of Grafton, his daughter or her fiancé, Edward Grey. We need to check very closely—not only on them but on the man Warncliffe, who was talking to Janice when the attack was made. He has a slight head wound. There is no way of being sure whether the shots were intended for him or for the girl.'

'What do they have to say?' asked Craigie.

'The girl, little or nothing. Warncliffe either has or pretends to have taken umbrage because Ned and I took charge at the scene of the shooting. There is something about a woman at the hotel, a Peke owner, whom Mike thinks is showing a lot of interest in Grafton, but it's not certain. Mike is lucky he didn't get more badly hurt, but he did a remarkable job. At least two people died in the Bugatti when it crashed—the local police are checking them. The third man, whom Mike calls Paleface, is the one we're after. Mike says he is...' Loftus gave Mike's description of the man which Craigie wrote down swiftly. 'Mike's in a small nursing-home,' went on Loftus, 'and Mark is watching Grafton. Ned went with Warncliffe and Janice to Warncliffe's flat.'

'Is Errol badly hurt?' asked Craigie.

'More in spirit than the flesh,' said Loftus. 'He'll be about again within a week. The Bugatti's burned out of all recognition, even the number plates. I've got the local people trying to recall the number of a Bug seen this morning, and we must check it up. My chief interest at the moment is Warncliffe. He's a cool customer, and he's in well with Grafton's daughter.

Second, I'm interested in the fiancé, an Edward Grey. Get Miller to put the tabs on him, will you?'

'Yes,' said Craigie. 'What are you going to do now?'

'Have a go at Warncliffe at his flat,' said Loftus. 'Wish me luck.'

He stepped out of the call-box slowly, walking towards Millan Road, which was situated on the West Cliff between the Cliff Royal Hotel and the Square. It was in a select residential part of the resort, and Loftus walked without haste, contemplating the large and small hotels he passed and here and there a block of flats. At the third block in the road he stopped. Redfern Mansions was a garish-looking block of buildings painted a bright yellow and set amid half an acre or so of newly laid lawns.

An automatic lift took him to the third floor.

Number 41, Warncliffe's flat, was at the end of a wide carpeted passage. Loftus's footsteps were deadened as he walked, and he reflected on the obvious luxury of the appointments. The rentals here would be high, suggesting that Warncliffe was wealthy.

Loftus pressed the bell.

Warncliffe himself opened the door.

His head was bandaged expertly, and he looked glassy about the eyes. On the promenade he had been aggressive and exasperated, and when Loftus said: 'I hope your head isn't aching too much,' he showed that he hadn't improved.

'My man's a first-aid specialist. And if my head's not aching, it's hardly due to you. Your attentions are enough to give me a pain in the neck.'

'Crude, but probably true,' said Loftus. He stepped through into a large, well-furnished lounge, where Oundle was sitting on a settee smoking and making a fine effort to converse with

Janice Grafton. Oundle was doing all the talking, and the girl sat opposite him, nodding occasionally.

She was worried.

And, Loftus thought, not wholly because she had an eccentric father who claimed to have lost papers she stated to be non-existent.

''Lo, Ned.' He smiled at the girl and at Warncliffe's invita-tion sat down. There were seven or eight comfortable chairs in the lounge with two settees, yet the room was large enough not to seem overcrowded. In one corner was a large cocktail cabinet, against one wall was a walnut escritoire. The chairs were green, the wallpaper green-cum-beige, and the frosted glass of the wall lights merged perfectly. The carpet, too, was thick and toned with the rest of the room.

'Will you smoke?' Warncliffe proffered cigarettes. Loftus shook his head, and brought out his pipe.

'May I?'

'Yes.'

Warncliffe's full lips were curved in a smile that was not all of humour, but his mood was better.

'So you're careful, too,' he remarked. 'You either don't smoke, or smoke your own.'

Loftus arched his brows.

'It's a trade secret,' he said, 'but we have to be. Before we go any farther, do I have to remind you that but for us you would probably be very dead.'

'That's doubtful,' said Warncliffe sharply.

'I don't think so. We put the men in the Bugatti in a spot. They were after you, not my colleague. He shouted a warning which gave you a moment's notice of trouble. On the whole you've a lot to be thankful for and you're not showing it. May I know your full name?'

'Jeremiah,' said Warncliffe, and laughed. 'What is this, a

new system of interrogation? It isn't necessary; If I don't want to answer your questions, I won't.'

'I suspected as much,' said Loftus, applying a match to his loaded briar. 'We're going to be very frank.'

'That suits me,' Warncliffe grunted.

'Does it suit Miss Grafton?'

'You can take it so, yes.'

'I'd rather have her word for it,' said Loftus, looking towards the girl. Oundle, now smoking one of his own cigarettes, marvelled—and not for the first time—at the complete control of the situation which Loftus revealed.

Janice looked across at the big man.

Loftus saw trouble in her grey eyes—trouble in the tension at her lips, in the strain under which she was living.

'Do you mind what you hear?' he said.

'No.' Her voice was low. 'Jerry can speak for me, Mr. Loftus.'

Oundle, then, had given his name, or Warncliffe had got Loftus's name from the card of authority. But Loftus had a queer idea that his name had come too easily from her lips: that she had spoken it with a familiarity which suggested she had heard it frequently before.

Warncliffe's manner also suggested that he knew what he was doing, and gave Loftus the impression that he suspected that he was not a regular policeman. And Loftus remembered that the girl who had cannoned into Mark at Waterloo had known the Errols for Department Z men.

'Right,' said Loftus. He stood up abruptly, took off his coat and flung it over the back of a chair. 'Did you meet Miss Grafton by appointment today?'

Warncliffe eyed him evenly.

'What authority have you got for questioning me, Mr. Loftus?'

'Police authority,' said Loftus brusquely. 'A man known to be an enemy alien tried to murder you an hour or so ago. That is sufficient proof of your association with enemy aliens, and I need hardly warn you that internment camps have plenty of room.'

He did not shout, but there was a harshness in his voice greater than Warncliffe or the girl had heard before. The girl's hands tightened on the arms of her chair. Warncliffe's smile disappeared.

'What makes you think he was an enemy alien?'

'I'm not thinking, I know. Warncliffe, you may have some kind of statement to explain your position, and you've an opportunity of telling it to me. If you'd prefer the local police and a period of detention while inquiries are being made I don't mind. What I do mind is wasting my time. Now, let's have it. Was your meeting with Miss Grafton prearranged?'

Warncliffe sat down slowly.

'It was.'

'When was it arranged?'

'I have been meeting her by arrangement for some days past.'

'Why?'

'If you must know,' said Warncliffe icily, 'she prefers her father and her fiancé to know nothing of her friendship for me.'

'That's a possible explanation, but it doesn't fit entirely. I'm not interested in personal affairs, except in as far as they affect the activities of aliens in this country. I'll tell you what the man who shot you believes.'

'How can you?' flashed Warncliffe.

'Because I've means of finding out. He believes that Miss Grafton obtained the papers from her father, and passed them on to you. He believes that while you have them you are a danger to his country, and he proposed to kill you. With you dead he could safely operate against Miss Grafton. Does that make sense?'

'It could do,' said Warncliffe, and he looked towards Janice. Obviously the man was taken aback—and, for that matter, so was Oundle. Loftus stood up and stepped ponderously to the window. With his back towards it and frowning, he said slowly:

'You'll have to tell your story now, or later to a Tribunal, Warncliffe. The same applies to Miss Grafton. The cock-and-bull story that her father had no papers just doesn't convince. He has invented something of very great value. I want to know what it is, and where the relative papers are.'

'All right,' said Warncliffe, heavily. 'You can have the story—just as soon as I know who you are, and your official posi-tion. I'm taking no one on trust. Not even a man with a card from Scotland Yard which might be genuine, and might be forged.'

Loftus smiled for the first time.

'I can't say I blame you. Do you know the Scotland Yard number?'

'Of course.'

'Call it. Ask for Superintendent Miller, or Sir William Fellowes. Ask either of them whether I am working with their full authority.'

'Right,' said Warncliffe, stretching for a telephone on a small table close to his hand.

The girl sat back in her chair, with her eyes closed, long lashes sweeping her cheeks...

And Bill Loftus, by the window, glanced out.

The position he had taken up there had not been by chance. He was always prepared for anything, and in this affair he saw one essential factor: someone—Paleface to wit, and those working with Pale-face—wanted Warncliffe dead. That he had failed to achieve his object after one effort did not mean that he was reconciled to failure.

Thus Loftus saw a car moving slowly towards the block of flats.

It was an open touring car, and looked like a Lagonda. He could see that the driver was dressed in a light-grey suit, but he was more interested in the passenger, a man dressed in black and wearing a Homburg hat. What little Loftus could see of his face was pale.

Unostentatiously, Loftus slipped his right hand in his pocket. He was hidden from the street by the heavy curtain, but he could see outside. He saw Homburg was consulting what looked like a paper or magazine, and then he saw the man glance up. The scrutiny lasted for some seconds, before the man traced something along the paper on his knee.

He glanced directly at the flat; obviously he had been studying a window plan of Redfern Mansions, and had located the window he wanted.

Loftus eased his hand from his pocket, and his fingers were tight about a gun. He said so slowly that only Oundle heard his words clearly:

'Cut downstairs, Ned. A black Lagonda—get after it as fast as you can.'

Oundle nodded, and was out of the room before either of the others realised that he had started. The girl stared at the closing door, while outside the man in the Lagonda stood up and took something from a small leather case at his side.

Loftus roared:

'Lie on the floor!'

It was all he could do to warn them, he had to chance their obedience. He saw something small and dark curling towards the room, its direction accurate enough—and he saw that it was a hand-grenade.

He fired, deliberately.

A still target would have been easy enough, but in that fraction of a second Loftus knew that there was only one way to stop disaster at the flat—*and* yet let Pale-face get away. That might prove a wrong decision, but he made it then and there.

His gun made only a slight sneezing sound.

Flame stabbed, and the little dark sphere continued to curve towards the window. It was four yards away when the bullet struck it. Loftus turned and fell flat on his stomach. The girl was on the floor; Warncliffe, with the telephone in his hand, had one arm across her waist; he too was stretched out.

There was a *boom!* that deafened them for a moment, a gust of wind that sent the curtains flying towards the ceiling, a crash as the glass broke and crashed inwards. Pieces of dirt and debris hurtled through the air, and something struck against the glass of a wall-light, shattering it to a thousand pieces. And then silence—silence which seemed loud, for their ears were echoing, and they felt the physical reaction after the shock.

Loftus moved first.

His jacket had been blown almost off his back, and his hair was standing on end. He shrugged the jacket back into position, and reached the shattered windows. He was in time to see the Lagonda moving towards the first turning, with the black-coated man at the wheel. The man in grey was huddled next to him, apparently a victim of the explosion. The car gathered speed, while fast on its tail went Oundle, in the Talbot. Oundle appeared to be untouched, but a wing of the Talbot was smashed in, and the car might prove badly damaged.

There were voices coming from the other flats now, while

three A.R.P. wardens, complete with tin helmets and gas-masks which they were fitting hurriedly, rushed into sight. Loftus's lips curved grimly at the sight of them, as he turned back towards Warncliffe.

'Someone probably thinks we're being raided,' he said. 'We'd better think the same, unless we want a lot of publicity.'

'What—was it?' Warncliffe was breathing hard, but he was quite self-possessed and helping the dazed girl to a chair.

'A hand-grenade. You're not popular, Warncliffe, and Jeremiah suits you. Or wasn't he the apostle of gloom?' Loftus began to hunt round the room, in which chairs were overturned; smashed glass and ornaments were everywhere. He seemed quite cool and self-possessed, and might have been used to similar outrages all his life. He found his pipe and straightened up. 'Now,' he said. 'We'll have callers any moment, but before they come—did Miss Grafton steal her father's papers and did she give them to you?'

7

MORE MYSTERY

A s dishevelled as Loftus, and still clutching the telephone
—although the wire had been torn from the plug and
the instrument was useless—Warncliffe stared at the big man
and then did the last thing Loftus expected. He laughed.

'You'll do,' he said. 'No, certainly not.'

'Thanks,' said Loftus, and seemed to take the other's words
on their face value. 'Now we'll deal with the A.R.P. Division.'

He did not, of course, say that he knew anything about the
mysterious explosion when a warden and a policeman called.
In the next fifteen minutes it transpired that a spinster had
been looking out of her window at the car, and seen the
grenade thrown upwards. She had, luckily, turned away from
the window and was unhurt, although suffering from shock.
Most of the other front rooms had been empty: there were no
serious casualties, although there was little unbroken glass in
Millan Road.

In the next half-hour every explanation from a gas-main
leak to an I.R.A. outrage was put forward by someone, and

systematic inquiries were being made at every flat in the building.

Loftus interviewed the local inspector, who had been summoned hastily, told the inspector precisely what had happened, and in Warncliffe's hearing—for a telephone in another room was not damaged—the man rang up Scotland Yard for confirmation of the card of authority. It was given by Sir William Fellowes, and Fellowes asked:

'Is Mr. Loftus there now?'

'Yes, sir.' A dazed inspector, a comparatively youthful man who was not used to anything but small crime, looked at Loftus.

'I'll speak to him,' said Fellowes crisply.

'The—the Assistant Commissioner wants to speak to you, Mr. Loftus.' The inspector eased the neck of his uniform, then tugged at a small moustache as Loftus took the instrument.

'Thanks,' said Loftus. 'Hallo, William...'

'You can forget the humour,' said Sir William Fellowes, still crisply. 'Craigie's just been on the phone. Have you heard from him in the last half-hour?'

'No. What's developed?'

'Two deaths in the black-out last night,' said Fellowes. 'Both people of importance.'

'Who?'

'One a District Commissioner for National Defence, and a permanent official from the Home Office,' said Fellowes. 'They were shot in the country village where they're operating, and the news did not get through early. Shot in precisely the same way as the man at Waterloo, and with the same kind of gun.'

Loftus tapped his finger against the telephone, making an unnecessarily sharp noise in Fellowes's ear. 'Like that is it—things are waking up. Nothing else developed?'

'Isn't this enough?'

'I don't know,' said Loftus. 'Some permanent officials ought to be removed somehow or other, this might prove a public benefaction! Tell Gordon I'm coming up with Warncliffe's story, will you, and that it's going to help?'

'I'll ring him at once,' promised Fellowes, and rang down.

Loftus turned, finding the inspector by his side, a man obviously impressed and yet deciding not to be put off his balance by a stranger who could call an Assistant Commissioner at Scotland Yard by his Christian name.

'What do you advise about the—er—story to the Press, Mr. Loftus?'

'Suspected I.R.A. outrage in Bournemouth,' answered Loftus promptly. 'The driver of the car is believed to have looked like an Irishman.' He kept a straight face until the inspector went out, and the door was closed. In the dining-room—less equipped with easy-chairs but with enough for comfort—Warncliffe was regarding him with mingled amusement and astonishment—if Loftus read his expression aright. Janice Grafton was standing by the fireplace, and she seemed more composed than Loftus had seen her.

'You can handle situations,' Warncliffe said.

'It's a habit,' said Loftus. 'And authority, of course. I hope you noticed that. Well now, the interlude's over, and that's another piece of evidence that our enemy alien doesn't like you. It was the same man of course.'

'Why on earth didn't you stop him?' demanded Janice. It was sheer nonsense to let him get away.'

'My dear girl, try to get some sense in your noddle,' Loftus said. 'I don't want to be rude, but you're acting like a school-girl, and you should know better. If it's an act, drop it. I don't like amateur actresses, and in any case they're apt to flop.'

It was abominably rude, of course, and she would have

been justified in losing her temper. Instead she looked at him steadily for some seconds, and then a smile curved her lips. 'Very well,' she said. 'Jerry, isn't it time you told Mr. Loftus something?'

'I'm still anxious to know who he is,' said Warncliffe.

'Unofficial police,' answered Loftus promptly. 'Warncliffe, you know as well as I do that my name's familiar to you, and you think you know who I'm from. Stalling won't get you confirmation, but a straight story might. Let's have it.'

'Sit down,' said Warncliffe, slowly. 'It's a long one.'

Loftus sat.

The other man talked, easily enough but at times stopping as if to marshal his thoughts. The earlier part of his story was interesting but little more. He was a reasonably wealthy bachelor who disliked London, and had spent most of the past four years travelling through Europe and the Near East. His favourite hobby, photography, included work by night, and consequently he was interested in lenses of all kinds. Professor—a courtesy title—Grafton was also interested in lenses, and the two men had exchanged notes for some time.

'Then,' said Warncliffe, quietly, 'Mr. Grafton developed a theory that he was being robbed, and watched all the time. He's always been subject to delusions'—Warncliffe glanced towards the girl, who nodded—'and he's always been careless with his experimental papers. He lost some figures about a lens which he developed for night-photography and accused me of stealing it. I had marching orders. At that time Jan and I were—well, we'd more or less reached an understanding, but she seemed to take her father's part. I flew off in a temper, and...'

'How long ago was this?' asked Loftus.

'About eighteen months.' Warncliffe paused. 'I spent the next year—more or less—roaming round the Scandinavian and middle-Europe countries, getting back after the war had started and then not without a lot of trouble. I was in Poland,' he added casually.

'And you got out,' said Loftus. 'The frontiers weren't watched as well as they might have been.'

'Have it your own way. At all events I came back here, and sought Jan out. She had become engaged meanwhile to Teddy Grey. Have you met him?'

'Not yet.'

Warncliffe shrugged.

'It's not for me to say anything about Teddy, he means well. We were by way of being friends—he introduced me to Janice, in point of fact. And he wasn't interested in anything the Professor was likely to invent, although he was prepared to back him financially...' Warncliffe broke off, and Janice said quickly:

'You can speak bluntly, Jerry. Dad gave his consent to the engagement conditional upon financial backing, and he got it. To the tune of ten thousand pounds,' she went on. 'That of course made Teddy one of the family, more or less.'

'Continuing to speak bluntly,' said Loftus, 'you'd give a lot to back out of the engagement, wouldn't you?'

'I would,' said Janice.

'And money's the obstacle?'

'Obviously.'

'There's more chivalry and filial duty in the world than I thought,' said Loftus. 'Right, I know where we are so far. What goes next?'

Warncliffe lifted his hands helplessly.

'The queerest business imaginable, Loftus. I've been seeing Jan on the sly for some weeks, and she told me that she was worried about the Professor. He had more frequent attacks of hallucinations, turned against everything and everyone—Grey excepted—who were about him, and was visited by several mysterious individuals who refused to give their names to anyone but Grafton. This was when they were living at Epsom, in a small house. For some unknown reason, the Professor decided to move down here, and I took the furnished flat. A week ago Jan heard her father telling Grey that he had perfected an invention that would prove the best secret weapon of the war. Jan told me—the next day I was nearly run down in the Square. Do you know it?'

'Yes.'

'I was almost bowled over the next day, outside the flat,' said Warncliffe. 'Then I had a telephone message telling me to get out of Bournemouth. Of course, nothing could have made more sure that I stayed. Two bruisers tried to push me over the cliff yesterday, and it's luck plus a little mountaineering experience that kept me alive. Today—well, you know all about today.'

Warncliffe stopped, and his expression suggested that he knew Loftus would not believe it. Loftus pursed his lips, and said easily:

'Do you drink whisky?'

'What the devil will you ask next?' demanded Warncliffe. 'I prefer beer, but...'

'Precisely what I was driving at,' said Loftus. 'I've a thirst as long as my arm.'

'We'll soon put that right,' said Warncliffe.

He stepped to the bell and pressed it—and almost on the instant the door opened. The man who entered was unusually short, but nearly as broad as Warncliffe. He was grey-haired, with a bald patch the more obvious because of his stature, and his features had the cold regularity of a good-looking man who would never be handsome. There was nothing remarkable about his face unless it was the immobility of his features. His lips, well-shaped but thin, hardly moved as he spoke.

'Yes, sir.'

'Some beer, Paul.'

'Very good, sir.' Paul went out as quietly as he had entered, and Loftus realised that the silent movement was another queer thing about the man. He raised his brows at Warncliffe, and said:

'Where was he during the shindy?'

'Somewhere in the background,' said Warncliffe offhandedly. 'I told him I didn't want to be disturbed.'

'And he didn't trouble to find if you were all right during the bombing,' said Loftus dryly. 'He's well-trained.'

'I helped to train him,' said Warncliffe. 'What are you driving at?'

'You've been attacked by an unknown and for some equally unknown reason. Someone thinks you're playing an important part in this business, which concerns the Professor's latest invention. *Ergo*, the attempts on your life. But our enemy alien doesn't try murder without a good motive. He knows that you know something—something you haven't thought it wise to tell me. Consequently you wouldn't spread it around to anyone else. Yet there's been a leakage, and it might be through your man. I wanted to see the man—and quench my thirst.'

Warncliffe shrugged. 'Please yourself. You've had the whole story as far as I know it.'

'I haven't. My name was familiar to both of you.'

'Yes,' agreed Warncliffe, and Loftus was faintly surprised by the admission. 'The Professor again. He's mentioned a man named Loftus several times—and some Department or other at Whitehall. That's all I can tell you.'

'So-o,' said Loftus, 'you throw the onus on the Professor. It might work. We'll have a drink on it, anyhow.'

Paul came in, with a tray and four bottles of beer, and a soft drink for Janice. He poured two glasses of beer expertly, bowed, and went out. Loftus drank slowly, and apparently with enjoyment, and slipped in another of those unexpected questions.

'Do you ever write to each other?'

Janice nearly spilt her drink.

'You're uncanny,' said Warncliffe, and he seemed a trifle embarrassed. 'Yes, daily. We—er—make a habit of handing our letters to each other when we meet. I know it seems a lot of tommy rot, but it's a fact.'

'Accepted as such,' said Loftus lightly. 'I'm engaged,' he added off-handedly. 'And you two lunatics—assuming your story's true—can't see what's been causing the bother.'

'I can't,' said Warncliffe bluntly.

'Nor me,' said Janice frankly to Loftus.

'All right,' said the big man. 'We'll assume that the Professor has these papers concerning the new lens or whatever he's discovered. He's being watched by enemy aliens. They see his daughter hand you papers of some kind when you meet. You're known to have travelled about Europe a lot. They assume that you're connected with some kind of espionage, imagine the letters are scraps taken from the Professor's notes and consequently decide that you're best removed. Possible?'

'It—it's uncanny,' said Janice, and she was breathing heavily. Warncliffe stared—and then Loftus's voice hardened, and his expression was grim, accusing.

'It's not uncanny, it's fact,' he said. 'You may write love-letters, but you've also been exchanging the Professor's papers. Why?'

And he stared at them each in turn, while the silence in the room grew tense.

8

DARKNESS AGAIN

Warncliffe looked really taken aback, and the deep breath which the girl took was evidence that Loftus had gone very close to the mark. Warncliffe took out cigarettes, and his fingers trembled a little as he struck a match.

'How much *do* you know, Loftus?'

'Enough to be sure when I'm hearing the truth or not,' said Loftus.

'Well, I suppose it's useless to fool around much further. I've told you the truth, except about the letters—and that was half-true. This is going to sound like a lot of nonsense, but Jan's been picking up odd notes that Grafton's left in his room, and I've been trying to make sense of them. There is a lens he's invented, and the mystery end of the business has made me decide to have a cut at finding what he's got. I didn't like the sound of these strange visitors, and Jan imagined that one of them spoke in German. Of course we could have gone to the police, but it's her father.'

'Do you believe us?' demanded Janice, suddenly.

'Yes, up to a point. I'll believe you until I've proved you're lying, anyhow. Your consciences will look after you while I work on that basis. Have you no idea at all what the new lens is?'

'It's a darkness lens,' Warncliffe said.

'Meaning exactly?'

'Well—without getting technical, it's an improved night-camera as far as I can gather—something which will take a snap in the dark, or what we think is dark.'

'Such as the black-out?'

'Yes—there's always a certain amount of reflected and indirect light,' said Warncliffe. 'Generally any photograph taken in a poor light needs a carefully calculated exposure. This thing of Grafton's could enable anyone to take a snap by night as well as by day.'

'Far-reaching,' said Loftus. 'And valuable.'

'Look here, Loftus, are you suggesting we're conspiring to rob the old man?' Warncliffe protested. 'I...'

'I'm suggesting nothing,' said Loftus. 'If I were you, I'd be grateful that you haven't had to tell this story to the police, they'd probably decide a cell was the best place for you. Or have you forgotten it's war-time? For the rest, I shall have to have you watched. If you take my advice you'll stop taking notes from the Professor, Miss Grafton, and you'll both lay as low as you can. Our enemy alien won't stop trying. Understood?'

'I suppose it's unavoidable,' said Warncliffe reluctantly.

'It is. Believe it or not, there are people watching the flat right now. Miss Grafton, it might be an idea if you went to see whether your father has come round after his collapse this morning.'

He nodded, and stepped to the door. Without another word he went out, and slowly down the stairs of the flat. Deliberately he had left them on a mental stretch, for he wanted to find what their reactions were likely to be.

There was no car outside, but two men lounged at the far end of the street. Loftus knew that Craigie had hurried to get them there since their phone talk. Probably they had flown from London; certainly he could rely on them giving Janice Grafton and Jeremiah Warncliffe close attention. He recognised both agents although he made no sign. Turning left from Millan Street, he walked to the Cliff Royal Hotel.

Mark was there.

The Professor had come round, but had taken to his bed. Edward Grey had been in the house most of the time, and seemed in a bad temper. He was in the lounge, and Mark pointed him out to the big man, who frowned thoughtfully as he looked at Grey and then away.

There was much in common, as far as appearance was concerned, between Grey and Warncliffe. They were both of an age, probably in the early thirties. Both were medium-coloured, both physically impressive, probably well-educated. The main difference was in Grey's rather petulant expression. He looked like a man who had been spoiled all his life.

In Mark's room Loftus explained what was necessary, and:

'You'll have someone to give you a hand before dark, Mark; Mike will be out of action for a bit. You stick to the Professor. Tommy Lister is looking after the girl, and Jock Allison is on the tail of another boy-friend of the lady's. Whoever comes down to make the quartette wins the Grey bird. All right?'

'Yes,' said Mark, scowling and drawing a finger along his straight nose. 'I suppose it's got to be. I also suppose something will happen one day.'

Loftus grinned. 'One day, perhaps. Keep your eyes very closely on the Professor. He might prove a surprise number before this show's over.'

'He'll probably still be in bed.'

'All right,' said Loftus, 'be miserable if you must. I am going to London to worry about two men who died last night. Mark...'

'Hm-hm?'

'The danger comes after dark,' said Loftus soberly.

He went downstairs to the telephone—a call-box in the hotel—and phoned Craigie. For the past hour he had been expecting word from Oundle, and he hoped that Craigie would have some news. Apart from a report from a Bournemouth agent that Oundle had sent out a radio call for help, and was getting it, there was no news. Loftus felt his anxiety rising, remembering the ruthlessness of the attacks so far and the thoroughness of Ned Oundle. If it were possible to get word through, Ned would do it.

Just what did his silence mean?

Loftus tried to force the thought to the back of his mind, but failed. He was very uneasy indeed.

From the moment that Loftus had snapped the order to get outside and follow the Lagonda, Ned Oundle had been active. Too active, he considered. He took most things as they came, but too much had come too quickly.

To reach the front door and to be faced with the explosion had been bad enough in itself. Oundle, with a split-second in which to act, had retreated along the wide hallway of the flats and, since the bomb had exploded at the first-floor level, had felt nothing more than the wind. Outside, the Talbot had been in going order, although damaged. He had contrived to get in the wake of the Lagonda, after seeing the man in black push the other in grey along and then jump from the rear to the driving-seat.

The chase had led, leisurely enough, through Bournemouth.

Within three minutes Oundle had radioed his request for help to the local agents. He had proposed to keep the Lagonda in sight until one of the others had caught him up; the other, in a car which Pale-face would not recognise, would do the following.

Excellent, thought Oundle, in theory.

He had actually seen a Department car—rather a Lancia— driven by one Wally Davidson, whom he knew well. And within three minutes he had seen Wally swerve across the road to avoid a pedestrian, and crash into a shop window. He would have to keep on the tail of the Lagonda until his second man arrived.

He did not arrive.

Oundle followed the Lagonda, still at a leisurely pace, along the Christchurch-Lyndhurst road. Pale-face was inexplicable, for he drove across and about the New Forest, from Lyndhurst to Ringwood, Ringwood to Fordingbridge, back to Cadnam, Cadnam to Romsey and then back to Brockenhurst. There the man in black and his companion, who apparently was not badly hurt, had stopped for lunch.

Oundle's disquiet increased when, after lunch—and about the time that Loftus had started for London—Pale-face and his companion left the small hotel, and started driving again. From Brockenhurst they went along the Christchurch road, apparently back towards Bournemouth.

The Lagonda was travelling at something under forty, when it suddenly drew away from the Talbot. In a few seconds its speed doubled, and a few hundred yards ahead at cross-roads with trees and high hedges lining them.

The Lagonda disappeared.

Oundle swore, coming as he did on the cross-roads

without much warning, and tried to see which way the other car had turned. He saw the back of it, towards the right, swung the wheel and took the corner on two wheels.

The road was narrow and winding.

It led, Oundle believed, towards Burley, and in a few minutes, driving across barren countryside and with the Lagonda in clear sight, he saw the skeleton of the Territorial camp which had been dismantled at the beginning of the war. It was Burley, then.

The Lagonda kept its distance.

Both cars must be running low on petrol, and Oundle felt anxious lest he was the first to run out. He could not stop for refuelling, although he carried ample ration-vouchers in his pocket, unless Pale-face did the same.

Then an Austin Seven came towards him.

The small car seemed miles away when he first sighted it, but he was level more quickly than he realised—and then he heard the *tap-tap-tap* from the back of the small car, saw the yellow flame preceding machine-gun bullets, and felt the impact of them on the battered offside wing. He did not try to slow down or swerve, but drove straight on. He felt both surprise and relief when he found the four wheels holding the road.

He glanced behind him.

The Austin had stopped, and was turning in the middle of the road. The Lagonda was moving as fast as ever, close to Burley village. It swung right, however, and started to go across the common again. Oundle had to follow.

With the Lagonda in front, and the Austin behind.

The road was winding a great deal with steep banks on either side. It was difficult to operate the radio-transmitter, but the circumstances made it imperative. One-handed, he switched on; but he heard no atmospherics, the instrument sounded dead.

It *was* dead.

The aerial was carried on the running-board, and with a sickening sense of hopelessness Oundle realised that it had been shot through. He was alone, there seemed no other traffic on that road leading across the forest except the Austin on his tail and the Lagonda ahead of him. Dusk was beginning to fall despite the early hour, and was made worse by heavy banks of cloud coming from the sea.

Darkness. Black-out.

Could these people see in the dark?

Was that the object of the long, apparently senseless run? Had the Lagonda driver been keeping him at a distance in order to make use of the darkness?

'It looks,' said Oundle aloud, 'just like that. And perhaps, Bill, you'll tell me what to do if the Lagonda stops suddenly.'

Loftus was a long way off.

Pale-face was uncomfortably near, and so were the occupants of the Austin. It came to Oundle that the machine-gunning had been intended to get his aerial and miss the tyres and him—that he had been lured deliberately into this position, on one of the wildest parts of the New Forest, so that darkness should fall.

And in darkness—what?

9

BY MESSENGER

Ned Oundle believed that he knew the New Forest well, but until that day he had known nothing of the loneliness of some parts of it, and had not realised that there was so little traffic, that there were such extensive stretches of moorland, bleak and wild, relieved neither by trees nor ponies. He was not sure what part of the Forest he had reached, for twisting and turning corners at speed had made it impossible for him to read the signposts. The last village had been Burley, but that meant little.

'And this,' said Oundle to himself as he coasted along behind a Lagonda at little more than thirty, 'means less. I wonder what they'd do if I tried to pass them?'

He spurted; but the Lagonda drew away, while the Austin contrived to keep within easy distance.

Oundle faced the facts philosophically. By a cunning manoeuvre he had been stranded—and his chief problem was deciding whether to try to get away, or to wait for developments. His inclination, now that he was used to the prospect of a forced meeting with Pale-face by dark, was to wait; on the other hand, he needed to get word through to Loftus.

Then Oundle discovered a further angle in the ingenuity of Pale-face. The Lagonda slowed down whenever it neared cross-roads or side turnings, and the Austin gathered speed. At those moments little more than forty yards covered all three cars. Oundle tightened his lips after passing three turnings, and then swung the wheel for the fourth.

The Austin was no more than ten yards behind.

Even as he turned the wheel, Loftus heard the ominous *tap-tap-tap* of the Tommy-gun which was being used against him, and felt the impact of the bullets on the body-work. He was not hurt, but if he persisted in his effort to swing off the road he would be. He straightened the wheel, and the gunning stopped.

Oundle wiped the perspiration from his forehead.

The bank of clouds was now above him. Northwards there was a strip of comparatively clear sky, shedding a little light, but for the most part the sky was overcast, and dusk was premature. He switched on the lights permitted by law; the Lagonda did the same, as did the Austin.

The darkness worsened until it was only just possible to see the hedges and, here and there, a tree which was no more than a vague, skeleton shape against the sky. The red light of the Lagonda showed occasionally ahead of him, the faint white light from the Austin was behind. His own dimmed headlights showed on a few yards of road ahead of him.

Then, abruptly, his engine missed fire. The car ran for a few yards, but the engine missed again and stopped completely. Tight-lipped, Oundle sat back in his seat. His right hand was in his pocket, tight about the butt of a gun. But he knew that it would be of little use. He could see nothing beyond the range of the headlights, while the others probably could see in the darkness.

The red light of the Lagonda was no longer visible, nor was the whiter light of the Austin. Darkness and silence surrounded him, the quiet of the night seemed a menace in itself.

'I think,' Oundle said in a voice very unlike his own, 'that I'll take a walk.'

'I disagree,' said a voice from behind him.

Oundle started. He had heard and seen nothing, but a man was within a yard of him. He turned his head, but the voice came again, sharply.

'Switch off your lights.'

Oundle hesitated, but obeyed.

The blackness was complete, and he could see nothing even when he turned his head and tried to locate the speaker. He felt the utter hopelessness of his position, and yet had one reassuring thought. Had they intended to do murder, they would have shot him by now.

'Remember,' said the speaker softly, 'that I can see you perfectly, Oundle, as well as if it were daylight. You will do precisely what I tell you, or you will not live to do another thing. Now! Get out of your car on the far side.'

Oundle opened the door, finding the handle by touch. He would not have believed such utter darkness possible. It seemed to envelop him like a shroud. He shivered, and it was not entirely due to the cold, although a wind was whistling across the moors.

He reached the roadway.

He stopped abruptly, for from the darkness an invisible hand gripped his right wrist, and his hand was drawn from his pocket, his fingers prised away from the butt of his gun. Other hands ran over him from head to foot, and a second automatic which he carried in a shoulder holster was removed. He could feel the hands but could not see them.

His heart beat fast.

'Come with me,' said a man gruffly.

It was not the first speaker, and there was an accent in the second voice which suggested that the man was ill-educated, but as English as Oundle. A hand gripped his forearm and the man at his side walked sharply and steadily along the road. His escort walked as firmly and surely as he would have done by day.

'All right, stop,' growled the other. 'All ready, sir?'

'Both of you get in.' It was the softer voice this time, and although he could not be sure, Oundle believed it to be from Pale-face. But Oundle had little time for thinking, for he was helped into a car—almost certainly the Lagonda—and his escort sat beside him. Something hard was pressed against his ribs.

In darkness and without lights the car started smoothly.

Oundle felt it taking corners, and travelling round bends but there was nothing he could see ahead of him, and his sense of the uncanny increased, grew almost frightening. Now and again, when the lights of an approaching car were seen, the driver switched on—but that was rare, for the most part it was a ghost car, travelling through a blackness which no normal man could have negotiated. It was uncanny, yes, and even frightening—but it was fascinating.

But like all things, it grew monotonous. He had no idea how long he had been travelling, but suddenly the car swung on to a main road, and traffic was comparatively thick. Lights were everywhere, and those of the Lagonda were on all the time. The pressure against his ribs increased, a further warning.

The Lagonda turned off the road and ran on for perhaps

five minutes, then stopped. The driver climbed out, and Oundle heard the creaking of gates as they opened. The lights were off again, but they went along a drive swiftly, and pulled up slowly.

'Get out,' ordered the man next to him.

Oundle obeyed, stumbling on the gravel. He regained his balance as the man with the thin voice said sharply:

'You have seen a demonstration, Oundle, which should satisfy you that you are quite helpless. Go back to Loftus, and tell him what has happened. Tell him to withdraw his men from the Graftons, Warncliffe and Grey. Tell him he is doing no good by fighting, but only harm. You understand?'

'Ye-es.' Oundle was so startled and at the same time so relieved that he stared through the darkness like a man dumbstruck.

To the village of Grayling, in Hampshire, a section of the Home Office had been evacuated during the first days of the war, and there taken root. The Manor House, which had long been on the market, had been bought—not rented—by a generous Government, and in the locality scurrilous tongues suggested that a house which had been unsaleable during peace-time had been bought at an extravagant price by a Government Department, one of whose officials was a first-cousin of the owner.

Such things, of course, were only whispered.

Moreover, as the weeks had passed, the scurrilous tongues ceased to wag—and with good reason. Grayling was a small village, with only half a dozen shops and two hostelries. What few county folk lived near by did a little hunting, a little fishing in the Tess, and considerable shooting in the extensive rough-land. They omitted, however, to patronise the Grayling shops, and bought either from Winchester or London. The villagers and the farmers from nearby gave what prosperity there was in Grayling until the war.

The outrageous purchase of the Manor House was at first a topic of conversation, and then of satisfaction. For it was a large building, with some twenty-one bedrooms, and others for servants—and a large staff was brought down from White-hall. Grayling woke up one autumn morning to find its popu-lation increased by nearly a hundred souls—mostly youthful souls. Beer was sold in far greater quantities than ever before, cigarettes were out of stock within three days, other sales increased in proportion. Moreover, the controlling official, Sir Arbuthnot Wilson, gave instructions to the resident cook that what purchases could be bought locally should be.

Grayling thrived.

Grayling, in fact, was ninety-eight per cent solid for the Government, and the only remaining Socialist was the local vagrant-cum-poacher-cum-oldest inhabitant, none other than Sammy Doe.

Sammy was a practising Socialist rather than a political one, and had no genuine reason for complaint. But he did complain, and he talked at the Green Swan of the outrages of the Government, and the fact that Sir Arbuthnot Wilson ought to be shot—and lo! on a raw morning in early spring Sammy Doe stumbled across a body.

A dead body.

None other than Sir Arbuthnot Wilson's, who had been shot.

It did credit to Sammy that he went immediately to the police and admitted that he had been snaring rabbits—or more accurately collecting them after setting his snares the previous night—when he had discovered the body lying beneath a pile of leaves in a little-used covert half a mile from the Manor House. The local police had summoned those from Winchester, and there had been much ado before the search party which started out to look for evidence or clues, discovered a second body.

This time it was of Lord Horley, District Commissioner for Home Defence for the Mid-Southern area—a murder likely to arouse even greater sensation than that of Wilson's. At first stunned by the importance of their discoveries, the Winchester police had delayed contacting Scotland Yard, with the result that an obscure agent of Craigie's had heard of the killings, discovered both men had died from bullet wounds in the temple, and had advised Craigie. Both wounds had been caused by small-bore guns of the air type.

Craigie told Loftus this, and:

'There's no apparent reason for either murder. Both men were well known and reputable, and it looks as if they might have been killed as an example of the efficiency of this new weapon. But it's our job. You've a *carte blanche* with the locals. Get down at once, will you?'

'Yes,' said Loftus, who had been in London for no more than half an hour. 'Anything from Oundle yet?'

'No. Wally had a car smash just after sighting him in Bournemouth, and Carruthers missed him somehow.'

'Huh. You'll phone me if word comes through.'

'Of course,' said Craigie.

Loftus nodded, and went out. Craigie looked at the door as it slid to—operated from a button-panel on Craigie's desk, for no man could get into that long room without Craigie knowing—with his eyes narrowed and worried.

The killing in darkness was desperately worrying.

Why was it happening? Why kill an unknown alien, an Englishman with a list of a dozen convictions for petty crimes

—that was the man who had followed Loftus from Scotland Yard—and, above all, why kill Wilson and Lord Horley?

The police had failed to make progress.

They had not been able to identify the alien, and the billiards chalk clue had so far been useless. The other man, known for some obscure reason as Harry the Bat, had been released from his ticket-of-leave obligations three months before, and as far as the police had known, had led a blameless life thereafter. But he had followed Loftus in the dark—and been killed apparently because he had allowed Loftus to realise that.

But why?

The weapon itself could be deadly enough, but why was it being used in these 'small' murders? Craigie would have preferred it had there been some obvious reason, had any of the dead men been concerned with espionage, or even with the War Office. The attempt to reconcile what seemed like 'private' crimes with the existence of a weapon which would be invaluable in the war was the difficult task.

No further news had come from Vania.

No word, for that matter, had come from any source about the invention which countered darkness. That developments were brewing was certain—and Loftus was as worried as Gordon Craigie when he went downstairs from the Department Office, using the side entrance from the big building and then turning left into Whitehall.

He had hired a car from Bournemouth for his journey, and had made it in fast time. He felt a little tired, for he had driven a lot that day, and many things had happened. There was one thing to be relieved about. Round the corner Spats Thornton was waiting, for Spats would be driving him down to Grayling, where he hoped to learn more of the murders of two gentlemen of importance.

Spats was there.

Immaculate in the half-light, with his Punch of a face red and even shiny, he was smoking a small cigar, and he wore a Homburg tilted at a rakish angle over his forehead. A caricature of a man was Spats Thornton, but as sound as they made them.

'News?' he asked.

'None of importance,' said Loftus. 'I'm getting in the back, and if you'll try not to drive on your brakes I'll try to get a nap.'

'Keep trying,' said Thornton solemnly. 'I... Bill.'

There was a steadier note in the last word, although his expression did not alter, and he continued setting the car in motion. Loftus said: 'Well?' without looking round.

'There's a car behind us, with a girl at the wheel.'

'How nice,' said Loftus.

'Don't be all of a damned fool,' said Thornton. 'She's starting off now. Driving a Bentley, and she looks as if she can handle it.'

'Not interested,' said Loftus, but he contrived to see the girl at the wheel of the Bentley.

From that distance she seemed small and petite. It might have been the half-light which also made her seem unusually pretty—but whatever it was, she looked pretty enough. And capable. One of the modern type, thought Loftus, who could drive as well as any man, and possessed even fewer nerves. She followed Thornton—who was driving his own Talbot—along Whitehall, the Mall, and eventually to Kensington High Street. There the traffic grew thicker and they lost sight of her.

'Well?' asked Thornton.

'She could be following us,' admitted Loftus. 'But there's nothing we can do about it, Spats. There isn't an agent who can follow her along; they'd never catch her up now, and we've no one stationed on this road. We just leave things to chance, and we keep hoping.'

Even when they had reached the Great West Road, and later when they were beyond Staines and scorching towards the flats over Blackwater Common, Spats could not be sure whether the twin orbs of light behind them belonged to the Bentley.

Spats made reasonably good time. He went through Winchester, lost his way then, but was lucky to find an illuminated road sign which he could read after stopping and craning his head forward. A few minutes later he was turning into the drive of the Manor, where the police were waiting for them.

Behind them came a second car.

But Thornton forgot that momentarily, and so did Loftus—who knew it as well as Thornton—for in the light of the dimmed headlights they saw a man standing rigidly near the wall of the big house. A man who was staring towards them, and who seemed struck dumb.

Thornton pulled up abruptly. Loftus left the car more quickly than seemed possible, for he recognised the man standing there and he did not like his attitude. He felt a wave of relief when Ned Oundle's voice came reflectively.

'Nice to see you, Bill. I've brought you a message.'
But even then Oundle was feeling dazed—and with good reason, for to find Loftus here, at the end of that nightmare drive, seemed to make the uncanniness of Pale-face sinister and threatening—and almost inhuman.

10
THE PACE QUICKENS

There was beer at the Manor, and other refreshments, and within half an hour Oundle felt a new man. While eating and drinking, he told his story, and he finished quietly:

'All joking aside, Bill, I've never had the wind up so much in my life.'

'So I gathered,' said Loftus dryly. 'They're clever, and they're trying to frighten us off. That suggests that they're not anxious to have us on.'

'Elementary,' grunted Thornton, who looked worried.

'Elementary or not, they wouldn't go to this trouble to keep us at a distance unless they were (a) scared, or (b) particularly anxious to impress us,' said Loftus.

'They've managed both,' said Thornton. 'I'm scared. So is Ned. So're others. Damn it, this eyes in the dark business is all right for cats, but...'

'None of which is humorous,' said Loftus, rubbing his chin. 'So you were the messenger, Ned, and you've brought the message. You've also brought confirmation of the fact that these people have cats' eyes. The problem is how far they can see, and whether the idea's any good from the air, for instance. If the range of vision is limited, it's not half as important as it will be if there's no limit. You didn't get a glimpse of Pale-face?'

'No.'

'What was his voice like?'

'You could say sibilant; he hissed a lot at the end of his words.'

'Hmm,' said Bill Loftus, and he stared thoughtfully ahead of him. 'That's a point, Ned, we'll have to put it to the test. The machine-gun was a Thomson-sub, was it?'

'It could have been an automatic rifle,' said Oundle. 'All I know is that it fired fast.'

'We still have to face the possibility that there are two lots of these people,' Loftus said, 'and if Spats is right, the girl who talked to Mark Errol on Waterloo followed us here in a Bentley.'

Oundle started. 'Did she, then!'

'It was no more than a guess,' said Thornton. 'I'm not even sure that she kept with us all the way.'

'She did, though,' said a woman from the door.

The room in which they were sitting was on the ground floor. It was spacious but drably furnished, and even the blazing coal fire in a large grate did not contrive to give it an atmosphere of cheerfulness. Shadows from the fire threw themselves against the half-panelled walls, some showing the apparently moving shapes of the beer bottles and the plate of sandwiches on the table.

The lamps were shaded, but gave a fair light.

The windows were heavily curtained, and there was a draught-excluder curtain at the door. This had deadened the sound of the door opening, had prevented any of them from hearing the noise of approach. Yet Loftus did not seem surprised as he turned his head at the sound of the voice.

Oundle's saucer-like eyes widened in surprise, and Spats positively gaped.

'I thought so,' said Loftus equably. 'Come in, sweetheart.'

The woman stepped farther into the room.

There was one thing remarkable about her: she carried an automatic in her right hand, and at the end of the barrel was the stubbed shape of a new-type Maxim silencer. She was dressed in a mink coat which must have cost a fortune, and an absurdly small hat, perched forward on her head, emphasised luxuriant dark-brown hair. The effect of the high collar of the coat and the low position of the hat was to make her face seem tiny—but it was smooth complexioned, the lips were small and very shapely, and there seemed an almost mischievous quality in her hazel eyes as she regarded them.

'The gun,' she said, 'doesn't make any noise.'

'Does it make a small hole, like an air-pistol?' inquired Loftus. He did not appear in the least put out, although the gun was trained on him.

Oundle and Thornton relaxed.

There were many uncanny things about this business, and Loftus was not the least of them. Sometimes he saw further than anyone else, Oundle believed—and both men were of the opinion that he had expected the girl's visit.

'It does not make a hole like a bullet from an air pistol,' said the girl gently. 'But it makes a nasty hole. Loftus, can't you take a hint?'

'I can try,' said Loftus amiably.

'You haven't tried much,' she said. 'You were warned the other night, and you were warned by telephone. Or didn't Mark Errol tell you about it?'

'All about it,' said Loftus. 'It's the worst of being an Englishman. I'm pig-headed. And'—he grinned—'I wanted to meet you. You had to turn up,' he said, and began to stuff his pipe unconcernedly. 'Is Pale-face a friend or an enemy of yours?'

Her lips tightened and the gleam disappeared from her eyes.

'Who do you mean?'

'Just Pale-face,' said Loftus. 'The man who habitually dresses in black, and...'

'Has he been—worrying you?'

'He contrived to worry Ned here, but not for long. We get used to these things. He's also worried others, but I wouldn't say that he has yet caused me much concern.'

'Apparently that would be difficult,' retorted the girl. 'Don't you know his name?'

'No. What is it?'

'Forster.'

'German?'

'Yes.'

'Nazi?'

'I think so,' said the girl. She had not relaxed, and she kept the gun trained on them. 'But that doesn't matter. You've been told often enough that if you interest yourself in this business you'll merely make matters worse.'

'There's such a thing as duty, or hadn't you realised that?'

'Don't talk like a fool. You don't help duty by running your head against a brick wall.'

'Except that sufficient hard heads might knock a brick out,' returned Loftus, still amiably. 'Sweetheart, your concern for me and my friends is touching, but it somehow doesn't ring true. Why don't you be sensible, and join forces? Obviously we've a mutual enemy in Paleface or Forster if you prefer, and we might go to many places together.'

'We will not,' said the girl, and she appeared to be quite

definite on the point. 'Loftus, you're inviting trouble, and you *can't* do anything helpful. You're quite useless in the dark, and it's by dark that you'll suffer.'

'I could train a cat as a guide,' said Loftus.

'Don't be light-headed,' she snapped sharply. 'We don't want to cause trouble to you or to Craigie, or anyone for that matter. But we're going to, unless you withdraw at once. I'll tell you something. A man met the Errols at Waterloo and was going to kill them. We would have stopped him, but Thornton was there, and they managed it themselves. Another man followed you from Scotland Yard the night before last, and died on your doorstep—when he was about to throw a bomb into your room. We took the bomb from him before he died, and we saw what happened afterwards. We *want* to help you— but it's got to be in our own way. Forster is necessary to us, in one way—but Forster is getting worried, and before long he'll give up the ghost.'

'It could be, I suppose,' said Loftus. 'I say, won't you sit down?'

'No thanks.'

'A pity,' said Loftus. 'Listen, angel, listen to me. You want the secret of this seeing in darkness business, and so does Forster. Doubtless if either of you get it you'll sell to the highest bidder. Or even to England, at a price. You'd like us to stand aside and let you carry on your private war with Herr Forster, and when one or the other of you has won, collect the dibs. I'd call it commercial minded. Wouldn't you?'

'Guessing won't help you,' said the girl sharply.

'You can give my compliments to your undoubtedly ingenuous employer, and tell him no.'

The girl pushed her free hand into a pocket of the coat—a pocket the others had not noticed before.

'You'll all regret it,' she said.

'I have doubts,' said Loftus.

'*I* haven't.' She might have been discussing any commercial deal, but seemed genuinely perturbed. 'You don't know what you're doing. This can be disastrous.'

'Not in the right hands.'

'We'll handle it all right.'

'I've doubts,' said Loftus, and smiled engagingly. But don't let me depress you. And if you really want to make a representation, why not speak to your Member of Parliament?'

'You're a bigger fool than I thought,' said the girl dispassionately, and she drew her hand from her pocket. She was clutching something, but the others had no time to see what, for she stepped back swiftly towards the door and switched off the light. For a split second the darkness blinded them, although it would be only for a moment or two before the firelight gave them all they needed to see with.

They did not have that second.

The door opened, and they felt the draught—and then she had completely disappeared. Loftus moved from his chair with startling speed for a big man, but although he reached the hall it availed him little for the darkness surrounded him. He fancied he heard the front door open and close, and he raced towards it with a torch in his hand. But the beam from the torch showed him only just a glimpse of the chair which had been put in his path. He had no time to avoid it, and he crashed downwards, the torch going from his hand and also going out. He felt Oundle strike against him and then Thornton brought up the rear and also sprawled. They were in a helpless jumble on the floor for at least half a minute, and when they had sorted themselves out and looked into the carriage-way of the drive they saw nothing and heard nothing.

* * *

The Winchester police were helpful.

They were impressed by the Home Office order which was sent to them by special courier, an order which put Loftus in charge of the investigations of the murders of Sir Arbuthnot Wilson, and Lord Horley. They—Loftus, Oundle and Thornton—saw the two bodies, which were lying in a small room of the Manor, and they recognised the bullet wounds.

But why had they been out at that time of night?

Both men had been seen in the Manor—where they had shared a living-room—at half-past ten on the previous night. It had been assumed that both were in their bedrooms, and as they had given no instructions for calling, they had been left—thought the servants—in peace.

Then Sammy Doe had found them.

Loftus interviewed Sammy, and was intrigued by the tall, spindly, gnarled old man who admitted defiantly that they had been near his rabbit-snares, that he believed rabbits were for the common man and no one had a prior right to them. He was proud of his poaching, and strong 'agin the Government'.

Not until after the interview with Sammy Doe had the authorisation come through from the Home Office for a search—and consequently the sales in the offices had remained locked. Loftus opened them, with Thornton and Oundle watching.

And Loftus exclaimed aloud, for the safes were empty.

One after the other was the same. No papers, no documents, nothing at all but the bare steel walls.

'Except,' Loftus said oddly as he straightened up from the last safe, 'this.'

And in his fingers was a metal disc, fairly new and a little larger than a halfpenny. On one side was a queer picture of two heads—both men—on one pair of shoulders.

Similar to that which had been found on the man at Waterloo Station.

'Things are moving,' said Loftus, and his expression was hard. 'Wilson and Horley were in something, and their reputations were probably ill-founded. If they were in this business others might be. The telephone, friends...'

He called Craigie, and was some time getting an answer, suggesting that Craigie was busy on one of the other lines. As he waited, Oundle and Thornton discussed the girl who had called and contrived to get away so easily. That trick of putting out the lights was an old one, of course; being able to see in the dark had made it doubly effective.

Loftus was thinking of the thing she had taken from her pocket, and wondering what it had been.

'Hallo, yes.' Craigie came on the line, and his voice was sharp. Loftus began to spell his name, but Craigie interrupted. 'All right, Bill. Get down to Bournemouth as soon as you can. Grafton's been kidnapped.'

'*What?*' shouted Loftus, and for a moment he looked as if he were going to lose his temper. 'Damn it, I left...'

'The lights in the hotel went out,' said Craigie, 'and all of our men were knocked out. They couldn't do a thing in the dark. The same applies to you.'

Loftus got himself under control.

'Ye-es. Things are certainly moving, Gordon. I've met Mark's Lady of Waterloo...' He talked for thirty seconds on that subject, and then switched to the discovery of the empty safes. Craigie's exclamation positively quivered over the wires.

'*Every* one empty?'

'There isn't a confidential paper in the place,' said Loftus. 'All particulars of arrangements for the Mid-Southern area are somewhere they shouldn't be. Check up fast on Horley and Wilson, will you? Private homes and what not.'

'I will,' said Craigie grimly. 'Bill...'

'Hm-hm?'

'Be careful,' said Craigie, and with those two words he said a great deal.

Loftus knew that Craigie was really alarmed.

He replaced the receiver, and turned to the others.

'Bournemouth, pronto,' he said. 'I'll have a word with the inspector upstairs.'

The Manor was used mostly for office work, and as a canteen. The staff which had been evacuated mostly slept out, although in the billiards-room there were a dozen people, either playing snooker, billiards—there were two tables—or cards at the small tables set in one corner. To get to the small room which the local inspector, a man named Mayhew, was using, Loftus had to cross the billiards-room. He had to find how long the papers had been missing—papers containing vital secrets, including the dumps for the storage of food, petrol and ammunition in that area, as well as plans indicating the vital industries and their plants.

There was a hum of conversation from the billiards-room as he entered, and the air was thick with a haze of stale smoke. Loftus stepped towards the far door, avoiding a man bending down to make his stroke.

And then, quite abruptly, every light in the room went out.

11

HOLD-UP

Loftus was startled, but less surprised than any of the others. He hesitated in a blackness relieved only by the faint glow from an electric fire, then put his hand in his pocket for his torch. The beam shot out across the room, and someone laughed on a high-pitched note.

'Easy goes,' said Loftus. 'These local plants have a habit of doing this. Make sure that the passage lights are out, someone.'

A stocky man in shirt-sleeves was nearest the door, and Loftus directed the beam of his torch so that the man could look out.

'All dark there,' he said.

Loftus thought swiftly. The sudden black-out suggested that the main switch had been touched, or that a main fuse had gone. He doubted whether this was an accident, and a moment later the door for which he had been aiming opened. His torch slewed round, and he saw the burly figure of Inspector Mayhew, a man with a remarkably prominent chin.

'What the devil's the matter?' demanded Mayhew.

'The lights have gone out,' said Loftus, and he raised a

laugh. During it he reached Mayhew, and he kept his voice low.

'How many men have you got on duty here?'

'Four.'

'It's not enough. There's more funny business, and I'd like every man and woman in the building questioned before they get out.'

Mayhew, with the Home Office order in mind, did not ask why.

'We can't stop them getting out in this,' he said.

'I know. But we can try. Ring for reinforcements, will you, and warn your men to be careful as they come along. They'll want reasonably good lights. I think you might give an order that all cars carry normal headlights.'

Mayhew stared. 'But regulations...'

'Don't matter this time,' said Loftus, and he said it convincingly.

'The nearest telephone's in the hall,' said Mayhew.

'I'll come with you. Gentlemen...' Loftus raised his voice, and in the dim-red glow from the electric fire he saw every face turn towards him. They looked odd, ghostly figures as they stood there, no longer started but taking the matter as a joke. 'I'd be glad,' said Loftus, 'if you'll all stay put until the word "go". No one to leave the room until the inspector or I give the word. Understood?'

A chorus of assent greeted him, and he followed Mayhew from the billiards-room. Mayhew also had a torch, and he reached the telephone two yards ahead of Loftus. Nevertheless it was Loftus who missed the *ting* of the bell as the receiver was lifted, and Loftus who said after a few seconds:

'Dead, is it?'

'It can't be. I used it half an hour ago,' said Mayhew.

But it was dead, and he tried the four lines in the house,

one after the other, to find that none of them showed any signs of life. The telephones had been cut off, the light was gone—and something of what it meant seemed to force itself on the inspector's understanding.

'Mr. Loftus, you don't think this is connected with the—er—trouble last night?'

'I do,' said Loftus. 'And if you take my advice you and your men travel in twos until daylight.'

He stepped to the morning-room, where he had left Thornton and Oundle, and he expected to find them waiting. He did not know why it came as such a shock, but he stood staring into the firelit room, where the empty beer bottles remained to throw their shadows—and from which Oundle and Thornton had vanished.

Mayhew's gruff voice broke across his thoughts.

'They've probably gone for the main switch.'

'Ye-es,' said Loftus, and under his breath he added: 'I hope so.'

'Do you know where it is?'

'Yes. Shall we go down?'

'We'd better.'

They passed no one—no startled servants, nor giggling maids. The house seemed deserted, although the regular staff was a dozen strong, and at that time of night they might all have been expected to be in.

'It's just along here,' Mayhew said, as they reached a narrow passage along which the beam of his torch showed eerily.

They reached the main switch, and did not need further telling that this had been done deliberately. Not only had the main switch been broken, but the whole switchboard—serving the domestic quarters, the hall and the landings, Mayhew said—had been wrenched from the wall. The wires were hanging loose.

'What do you think's happening?' Mayhew asked helplessly.

'I'm not prepared to guess. Where were your men stationed?'

'There should be one in the kitchen.'

'It was empty when we passed through,' said Loftus.

'He may have slipped away for a minute.' Mayhew went back into the large, white-tiled kitchen, fitted with electric stove and ovens, and with the walls faced with glass-doored cabinets. Everything was spotlessly clean, but on one stove there was a small saucepan of milk already warm. By it stood a jug, half-empty.

'Rogers!' called Mayhew, and again: 'Rogers!'

There was no sound. The silence and the darkness was about them, a darkness which seemed greater because of the beams from their torches.

'We'll try again, together,' said Loftus.

'Rog-ers!'

There was still no reply; the policeman stationed in the kitchen had disappeared, as completely as Oundle and Thornton.

'Where were the other men?' Loftus asked.

'One on the first floor, and the other in the—er—morgue.'

'We'll try that first,' said Loftus.

The small room where the dead men had been left until after he had arrived—Wilson and Horley were to be moved to Winchester the next day—was at the other end of the house. They walked through the dark passages, meeting no one and hearing nothing. Mayhew stopped by the door of the room, and his chunky face looked strained.

'He should be sitting here.'

'Outside the door?'

'Yes.'

'Let's make sure,' said Loftus.

Mayhew unlocked the door, and Loftus went through first. He shone his torch towards the couches where the two bodies had been lying when he had first seen then—and he exclaimed aloud, for the beam passed over the couches, but showed no bodies beneath the grey shrouds which had covered them.

'My *God!*' gasped Mayhew.

He had turned colour, and Loftus saw him put one hand against the wall, as if he needed physical support.

'Easy,' said Loftus. 'This is a lot of trickery staged to make us lose our heads. That's no reason why we should oblige.' He took a whisky flask from his pocket, and soon they felt better.

'The first floor next,' said Loftus firmly.

But the result was the same. The man who had been left on the landing—to make sure that no unauthorised person entered the floor, on which most of the offices of the hush-hush department were situated—had vanished like his companions. Every bedroom upstairs—the rooms belonging to the servants and to a few of the higher officials—was empty. But for themselves, and the men in the billiards-room, the place might have been empty.

Mayhew cleared his throat.

'That flask, Mr. Loftus...'

'You can drop the "Mr.",' said Loftus. 'Watch me closely, I might disappear too.'

Mayhew found a grin.

'It wouldn't be easy to spirit you away! What do we do next?'

'We adjourn to the billiards-room,' said Loftus, 'and take stock of what material we've got there.'

Loftus was thoughtful for the rest of the run down the stairs to the billiards-room, and Mayhew obviously had no inclination to talk. There was enough to think about, Loftus admitted—and the mystery of this sudden darkness, and the disappearance of twenty or more people, must have a reasonable explanation.

He opened the billiards-room door.

And then he had the biggest shock of the night, for the room was absolutely empty. The dozen men who had been there when he had left, and who had assented without question to his request for them to stay put, had disappeared.

In the reflected light of their torches the Department Z man and the inspector stared at each other without speaking—and both men felt the menace that there was in the house, both men wondered what shock was coming next.

It came from behind them.

A quiet, self-assured masculine voice, from a man whose presence they had not suspected.

'Are you satisfied, gentlemen? These floors are empty but for our three selves. Now, Loftus—we have to talk.'

Loftus turned slowly, without any sign of panic. He made out the vague figure of the man, who seemed to be a little more than medium height, and who wore dark-framed glasses. The glasses were clear against the vague, pale shadow of his face.

'Of course,' Loftus said.

'I hope you mean it. Inspector, I hope there will be no serious effects for you.'

'What...' Mayhew began.

He could not finish, for two men who materialised out of the gloom seized him, and one put a hand across his mouth. Mayhew choked, but he could do nothing to stop himself from behind dragged off—as quick and efficient a piece of work as Loftus had ever seen. Something approaching a smile twisted Loftus's lips.

'You're very effective,' he remarked.

'Very,' said the little man quietly. 'May I advise you that several others are near at hand, and that any attempt at violence on your part will come to a most unhappy end?'

'I'll take your word for it.'

'I'm afraid that isn't quite enough,' said the other.

Loftus felt his arms gripped, and the temptation to make a fight of it had never been stronger. He resisted it. His guns were taken, and his torch.

'We should be all right now,' said the man at his side. 'But you've rather asked for this, you know.'

'One of the things I know,' said Loftus casually, 'is that you're going to have a very big shock before you're very much older. Do you have a name?'

'Cartwright will serve.'

'Thanks,' said Loftus. 'Where do we talk?'

'In the morning-room,' said the man who called himself Cartwright. 'My sister will be there, and I know she will like to meet you again. You contrived to impress her.'

'The pity is that I didn't contrive to impress her well enough,' said Loftus.

'I have a list of instructions for you to telephone Craigie— one of the lines has been repaired, you will have no trouble,' Cartwright said. 'Provided Craigie accepts the ultimatum, there need be no trouble. If he doesn't—I should dislike,' said Cartwright slowly, 'to be responsible for the deaths of people who cannot help themselves. But the blame would be on your shoulders.'

Cartwright walked alongside Loftus with both hands in his pockets, but there were men behind them, and one carried a torch—presumably for Loftus's convenience. Loftus could just make out the man's profile.

It was sharp and clear-cut, the nose prominent, and the forehead very high. Dark hair was brushed well back from the forehead, and was sparse over the temples. The lips were pushed forward a little, and parted—Loftus fancied that the front teeth of the man Cartwright were slightly protruding. The chin was pointed, and the neck very thin. He was not wearing an overcoat, and his shirt and collar were white.

He opened the morning-room door.

The girl was standing with back to the fire, and with her hands behind her. She had taken off her fur coat, and was wearing a black dress reasonably long and consequently a little unfashionable. She looked lovely, particularly in the half-light from the fire. As far as he could see the only jewels she affected were pearls, on the high neck of her dress.

'Can't we have light?' asked Loftus.

'We have all we need, thank you,' said Cartwright. 'Sit down...' He indicated a chair, and Loftus accepted it. 'Would you care for a drink?'

'I would.'

'Garth, bring some—er...'

'Beer,' said Loftus.

'Beer for Mr. Loftus,' said Cartwright.

'I hope you'll drink with me,' said Loftus.

'I'm afraid not,' said Cartwright, who gave the impression of being a fastidious man, with his precise diction and his general neatness. 'I am a total abstainer, and so is my sister. Well now, have you seen enough to be convinced that you cannot possibly put up a useful opposition to us?'

'Am I convinced that I can't see in the dark?' asked Loftus. 'Not yet, at all events.'

'You're very foolish,' said Cartwright. 'We are serious in

everything we are doing, and you must be made to realise that. We do not want unnecessary bloodshed, but if it must come we will not shrink from it.'

'So you're preparing a blood-bath. No sane man would think of it. I hope you're sane.'

'I think I can say that I am. But there are some things which drive even a sane person to something which appears to be unbalanced. You must admit that every effort has been made to show you the uselessness of continued opposition.'

Loftus leaned forward, peering into the fire.

'I've had word of an absurd card pinned to Mark Errol's sleeve, and a crazier telephone call,' he said. 'I had the interview with your sister tonight, and frankly I think that was almost idiocy. Now you're offering what you think is proof...' He broke off and shrugged. 'Proof that you're quite crazy, I'm afraid that's the limit. My dear Cartwright,' he added impatiently, 'I'm representing Craigie, who represents the Government. A sailor doesn't take orders from anyone but his superior. Kill me and I will be replaced by others. Kill the others, you'll find someone else. You can't do it indefinitely, and each time to put someone away you tighten the rope about your neck. Already the police consider you a common murderer. They haven't much patience with ideals.'

Cartwright snapped: 'What ideals?'

'We-ell,' said Loftus, and he looked across at the man, whose face showed red in the firelight, and whose eyes seemed to be on fire themselves, 'they're reasonably obvious. You've a bee in your bonnet that the Government can't make the best use of Grafton's idea.'

Cartwright stared.

The girl leaned forward—she had sat on the arm of a chair—and said oddly:

'What makes you think that?'

'It fits,' said Loftus. 'Nothing else would. This absurd desire to force your will on Government officials suggests only an obsession. You underrate Government officials. Many are bad, and others blameworthy, but they exist in their millions, you know—even Craigie has hundreds of men and could call on hundreds more.' He spoke as if he were trying to influence a fractious child, and he continued to stare in the fire. 'You've helped me—or the Department—but you've also killed two reputable men, who...'

'Reputable!' snapped Cartwright. 'They were unspeakable swine. Neither knew what honour meant! Loftus, Wilson was taking a percentage—understand, a substantial percentage—from large retail firms who needed more than their allotted ration of foodstuffs, and were getting it. Horley was allowing that to happen in his district, and was taking money for other offences against the regulations which...'

'Were made by the Government,' said Loftus gently.

'Nonsense,' said Cartwright. 'The Government from first to last has mishandled the war, and...'

'You're going to put it right?' asked Loftus gently.

'I'm going to make sure they don't mishandle the greatest invention of modern times!' rasped Cartwright. 'A weapon so powerful that it will enforce peace, *and,* make the world safe from war. You think I'm mad. If a love of peace, a regard for my fellow creatures, and a hatred of the greed and avarice which has made this war inevitable is insanity—all right, I'm insane! But I'll tell you this. While I live, I will handle this weapon in the way I think best. *I've* got the secret of it, no one else. Grafton started something similar and he may even stumble across part of it, but the real thing is in *my* hands. Is that clear?'

'Yes,' said Loftus. 'What about Forster?'

Cartwright's lips tightened.

'He's a Nazi spy. At least a German, although he may be planning to sell to the highest bidder, if he gets what he wants. He won't get it, I've made quite sure of that.'

'He can see in the dark,' said Loftus evenly.

'He was lucky enough to steal...'

'Quiet!' snapped the girl, and her brother broke off, looking for a moment confused. Loftus leaned back and smiled—and his expression suggested tolerant amusement.

'Some of the glasses,' he said. 'Don't look startled, sweetheart, it was obvious that glasses explained the thing—fitted with a lens which defeats the darkness. Right?'

The girl said:

'You *are* uncanny. Jim, it's not safe to let him go.'

'Nice of you,' said Loftus grimly. 'I...'

He broke off, for the door opened abruptly. It flashed through his mind that his beer had arrived belatedly—but although the same man appeared it was not with beer. He was breathing hard, and obviously he had been running.

'What is it, Garth?'

Garth said jerkily:

'It's Forster, sir. With twenty men or more, and they're surrounding the house. They're armed, sir...'

12
BATTLE BY NIGHT

L oftus stood up abruptly, and the others were so startled
that they did not seem to notice it.

'How near is he to the house?' he demanded.

'Approaching along the two drives,' said Garth.

'Are the doors and windows on the ground floor
barricaded?'

'No, they...'

'They should be,' snapped Loftus, swinging round on
Cartwright. 'We can settle our differences afterwards, we've
got to join forces against Forster. Is that secret here?'

Cartwright said: 'Part of it.'

'How many men have you got?'

'Seven or eight.'

'Armed?'

'Yes, with automatics. But...' Cartwright straightened his
shoulders, and spoke on a higher note than before. 'I can
handle this, Loftus.'

'You can't,' said the girl quietly, and Loftus felt great relief.

'We're outnumbered, as we need every man we can get. Is it an armistice, Loftus?'

'For the duration of this, yes.'

'We can't ask more,' said the girl, and she stepped to her brother and gripped his arm.

'Jim, we've got to beat Forster.'

'But Garry...'

'Forget the buts,' snapped Loftus. 'Get those lights repaired if you can. We'll need all the Government officials there are on the premises, and all the light. How many spare pairs of glasses have you?'

'Two,' said Cartwright.

'I'd better have one,' said Loftus. 'Then...'

They heard a shout from the front door, and then the unmistakable *crack!* of a rifle shot. Another and another—and accompanying them were a series of dull thuds, telling Loftus that bullets were thudding against the door outside.

'Get moving,' he said sharply. 'Garry, make him see sense. I want my two men, and the policemen.'

'Jim!' The girl sounded desperate, and something in her voice seemed to jerk Cartwright out of the coma. He moved with surprising briskness, and took a small case from his pocket.

'Put these on, Loftus. Garth, release the two prisoners taken from this room and bring them here immediately. Loftus, if you try to get outside, you'll be shot. Garry, go to the back of the house and take control there. Use the gas if necessary.'

'*What?*' exclaimed Loftus.

'A weak gas,' Cartwright said, 'and there's too much wind outside for it to take much effect tonight, I think. It might help. We're not unprepared.'

'What's happening now?' demanded Loftus.

'I have a man with a rifle at each major door, and they can see into the grounds,' said Cartwright. 'I was afraid Forster might locate us, but wasn't sure.'

'You should have had bigger forces,' said Loftus. 'Where's that good telephone?'

'It needn't interest you,' said Cartwright. 'I can't call more men in a hurry, and you're certainly not going to call the police. And don't'—he snatched a gun from his pocket, and the sight of the thin, somewhat ascetic-looking man with the gun would have been amusing at another time—'and don't try to use force. If you're going to help, help.'

Loftus tightened his lips.

'I'll need a gun for that.'

'You can't...'

Cartwright hesitated, and before he went on, the door opened and Oundle and Thornton came in. Neither looked the worse for wear, but both were surprised at the sight of Loftus.

Garth, a thickset, burly man, carried a gun.

'Those lethal weapons, Cartwright,' said Loftus firmly. 'We'll get rid of the Forster bunch first if you don't stand there all night. We can talk afterwards. It...'

Across his words came a heavy thud. Another and another. He knew what it was, and from Cartwright's expression it seemed that the smaller man did.

There was a battering ram at the front door.

Cartwright snapped:

'Return their guns, Garth! Loftus, I am relying on you and your friends to keep the front door safe.'

He swung round and hurried from the room, while Garth took Loftus's automatics from a capacious pocket, then Oundle's, then Thornton's. From another pocket he began to take torches, and Loftus stepped into the hall, speaking as he moved.

'Set the torches so that they converge on the front door, Garth—put them on chairs, or something about waist-high. We've declared a truce, the mutual enemy being at our gates.'

Almost absentmindedly he put on the glasses as he reached the darkened hall. Odd that he should be so preoccupied with his thoughts that he should not be on edge when about to try the spectacles. He admitted afterwards that it was not until he got them on that he realised there was anything unusual in him wearing them.

But as they went on he forgot everything but the glasses in front of his eyes. He looked along the hall, seeing everything in a faint blue light. It was not bright nor garish, and it was not to be compared with day, *but he could see everything* clearly. Even the small panes of glass in the door, which was being battered from outside. Even the small pieces of carving in the oak-panelling of the hall. *Everything* was visible in minute detail, clear-cut and strongly marked.

It was then that he realised one strange thing. There were no shadows.

He stood there like a man struck dumb, until Oundle's voice came in his ear.

'Busy, Bill?'

'I—sorry,' said Loftus. He had forgotten for the moment that the others could not see. 'The torches, Garth, quickly. Ned, the position briefly is that Pale-face, known as Forster, is attacking the other birds, known as Cartwrights, and that we're pro-Cartwright at the moment. If we get through, the earlier hostilities are resumed, presumably.'

'So what?' asked Thornton sepulchrally.

'Forster and company can see, so can most of the other fellows,' said Loftus, 'be it light or dark. Keep the beggars from breaking in through this door, and if they do break in, stop them getting farther along.'

'Right,' said Oundle.

But it was too late.

It would have been too late even before Loftus had wasted precious seconds with the glasses. There was a resounding crash on the front door, and then another. A crack that seemed to waken the dead, and then the door burst inwards, pieces of glass flying in all directions. Four men, holding on to what looked like a young tree, staggered into the room.

'The doors!' snapped Loftus.

It was action now, and he would always show to best advantage when the need came for heavy work. He slipped into a doorway, and the others followed suit, firing as they moved. Three of the four men crashed down in the porch. The other managed to dart back into safety, out of the light of the four torches which Garth had set so that their beams converged on the doorway.

Garth had taken up his position by one of the doors.

The Department men were each at separate doors, and for a moment there was a lull in the activities. From somewhere else there came the sound of shooting, and there was a muffled explosion which suggested that Forster and company were trying to blow their way through one of the other entrances. Loftus called quietly:

'Keep well under cover, fellows—ah!'

Almost on his words came the *tap-tap-tap* of a machine-gun from outside, and bullets began to spray into the hall. No one could cross the hall or approach the doorway without running into that barrage of lead—lead that meant death.

With the glasses on, Loftus could see in the poor light from the torches, although not so well as with the naked eye for there was a bluish tinge to everything. Suddenly the lights went out. Bullets struck each of the torches and they clattered to the ground.

Then Loftus could see clearly.

The spurts of yellow flame were coming, although he could not see the muzzle of the machine-gun. He knew that only Garth of the others could see, and he could only call out to Thornton and Oundle:

'*Stay put, and wait for the word.*'

He stopped, and the shooting increased. Rightly or wrongly he imagined that the flashes of fire were coming nearer, and that they seemed longer. A moment later he saw the end of the gun, and he waited tensely.

The spraying bullets made a wider arc.

Loftus saw the man holding the gun—and then, not for the first time, a daring idea flashed through his mind. The men in the porch expected little opposition, and were growing bolder. In a few seconds they would cross the threshold, unless Garth started firing and drove them back.

He looked across the hall, and he grinned. For Garth was gesticulating wildly, and showing his open palms. He had no gun!

'Nice work,' said Loftus gently.

Oundle and Thornton kept quiet, as he knew they would and the men holding the Tommy-gun came bodily into the hall. Two others were just behind him, carrying ordinary automatics.

Loftus cried:

'Now!'

Thornton and Oundle fired towards the flashes from the gun, and the man holding it staggered and then fell backwards. The gun crashed to the floor, while the brace who had come in support darted back for the porch. Or started to. Loftus stopped there, getting one man through the head, and another through the waist. He stepped forward, safe—until the shooting started from the porch—except from Oundle and Thornton.

'Enough!' he snapped. 'Wait for it!'

And he moved.

He went for the gun that was lying ten feet away from him. He knew that the moment he was in line of vision the men outside would start shooting—and his knowledge did not let him down. As he went he felt bullets plucking at his clothes, felt one stir his hair. But he reached the Tommy-gun, stooped, lifted it, and then leapt for the doorway in which Garth was taking cover.

He made it.

Garth stretched out a hand to support him.

'Good work, sir...'

'Take my gun, and make it better,' said Loftus.

It was not his first experience with a Tommy-gun, and he did not expect it to be his last. He swivelled the gun round, and he opened fire, praying that the belt and ammunition holder had been refilled just before he captured it.

A burst of shooting brought a scream, and a man pitched forward into the hall. Loftus crept nearer knowing that with the Tommy he could keep the men at bay. He called: 'Heavy furniture across the doorway, fellows. Garth will direct you. Make it snappy, we haven't got all night.'

How they contrived to move a mountainous piece of Victorian furniture from a wall to the door and put it in position he hardly knew. He heard them swearing and straining, heard Garth giving instructions.

'A little to your right—right again—now back. Forward a bit, you've nearly got it—right!'

Loftus had stopped shooting for the past few seconds, and lent a hand. Shooting came, but the sideboard—or what looked like a sideboard—was nearly waist high, and by stooping low they were safe. They brought other, smaller stuff from the dining-room, and piled it on top of the sideboard, then reinforced the whole with heavy chairs and a settee, turned upside down. As they finished the shooting outside stopped.

'They've withdrawn to compare notes,' said Loftus. 'And we can do the same!'

And then suddenly the lights were switched on.

Loftus was startled, for the effect on him was the reverse of what it would be for Oundle and Thornton. He could see, but only dimly. He could see at a distance, but everything—near or far—seemed to be covered with a bluish mist.

He took the glasses off slowly, to find the others screwing their eyes against the light.

'Cartwright's found an electrician,' said Loftus. 'Keep right here, you two, and if there's another attack make sure it fails. Clear?'

'We'll do it,' said Oundle, and his saucer-like eyes no longer looked ingenious.

'You'd better,' said Loftus. 'Oh—don't go outside, it won't be healthy.'

'I'd gathered that,' said Thornton.

'Because Garth has instructions to shoot you in the back,' said Loftus gently. 'Be friendly with Garth. He might even find you beer.'

He was moving fast as he spoke, and he went through the kitchen quarters, more concerned than he liked to admit about Garry Cartwright. He smelt the cordite, and knew that there had been plenty of action in the rear of the house as well as at the front.

The girl was wearing her coat again, and smoking a cigarette. Her hair was ruffled, but she looked as cool as when

Loftus had first seen her. She lifted a hand in greeting, and her smile had the mischievousness of a child.

'Hallo, partner!'

'Hallo yourself,' grunted Loftus. 'We've forced 'em back.'

'Yes.' She frowned. 'I'm not happy about it, they seem pretty strong in numbers.'

'Can't you persuade that damn'-fool brother of yours to telephone for the police?'

'Not in a thousand years. Anyhow, the line's been cut. You needn't worry—if he says it's a truce, he means it. But when it's over there's going to be trouble with the police—if you let them out. Is it wise?'

'I can handle the police and the Cartwrights,' said Loftus grimly. 'Where are they?'

'I'll show you. Look after things, Appleby.'

A tallish man, wearing suède shoes and dressed in a dandified fashion which was absurdly incongruous in the scullery where they were standing, nodded and smiled. He had long, dark hair which fell into his eyes, and his complexion was smooth and dark. He held an automatic as if used to it. So did three other men, while the linoleum-covered floor was littered with spent cartridge cases, and the glasses of many cupboards had been smashed to smithereens. The light was on, and none of the defenders was wearing glasses.

Garry Cartwright led Loftus to a cellar.

Crowded there like a lot of sheep were the men from the billiards-room, a dozen servants—the women in a smaller cellar on their own—while Mayhew and his three policemen were nearest the door.

Loftus told Mayhew what was happening, and he let the others know that there was an attack on the house, that every one of them had to take a share in the defence. He promised them that there would be no need for worry or anxiety once the police came from outside—and he prophesied that it would not be long before they did.

'But what are we to do?' a man called.

'Barricade places,' said Loftus. 'Four in a room at a time. Heavy furniture against all windows, and all doors leading outside.'

They dispersed quickly. Mayhew hesitated only for a fraction of a second, during which time his gaze rested on the girl.

'I'm taking these as orders, Mr. Loftus.'

'Good fellow,' said Loftus cheerfully, and the girl laughed as soon as Mayhew was out of earshot. Loftus looked at her with his head cocked on one side.

'You won't laugh if Mayhew gets hold of you, honey-bunch. Now where's this precious brother of yours?'

'At the side entrance,' said Garry Cartwright. 'Don't get too angry with him, he means well.'

'So do you, presumably,' said Loftus.

Before she could answer the house seemed to rock, the walls shivered, and a fire-extinguisher hanging in a wall-bracket crashed to the ground. A moment later there was a *boom!* that deafened them, a second, a third. The very floor shook beneath their feet, and the girl stared at Loftus, showing alarm for the first time.

Loftus said:

'High explosives, Garry, and that's not nice. Let's move.'

He ran for the stairs leading towards the ground floor, and as he went he wondered whether Forster had contrived to force an entry, or whether he was set only on destruction now that he had failed to get through with his first attack. He reached the servants' hall, and there he saw something of the effect of the explosion. The bombs had been thrown against the back entrance, and lying on the white-covered floor was the man named Appleby. What was left of his face was not nice to see.

Two other men were lying stretched out, and badly hurt.

While the barricade that had been hastily put up was gone, and through the dirt and debris and the smoke the first tongues of flame began to lick towards Loftus, he knew that the battle would have to end one way or the other before long.

It did not look like ending his way.

13

TRIUMPH FOR FORSTER

'This doesn't look so good,' said Garry Cartwright.

Even in the circumstances, and with the thought of the possible effect of the fire, which was starting, uppermost in his mind, Loftus had to smile.

'It isn't so good,' he said. 'Trouble is, young woman, you've put us all in a spot. Your own people, a dozen of the hated Government officials, servants and my trio are liable to suffer badly for this escapade.'

'It can't be helped,' she said. 'We didn't expect Forster to trace us here.'

Forster's men undoubtedly surrounded the Manor. He might have a dozen with him, or even more. It was reasonable to suppose that he had more than one machine-gun, and as reasonable to assume that he was able to see in the dark. Which meant that it would be impossible to get out, for any sortie would mean ruthless gunplay.

He was taking chance enough as it was.

The Manor was a mile and a half from the village, and on a quiet night it was likely that the shooting would be heard.

Certainly flames would be seen if they reached any proportions. There were lights blazing from some of the windows, for the niceties of black-out had been ignored; any casual passer-by might see that, and report. In fact help *might* come at any moment.

And might not.

Loftus straightened up after putting the unconscious man in the passage, and saw that the girl had gone. He heard hurried footsteps. Mayhew and a policeman came towards him, and Mayhew's face held more than a hint of alarm.

'Loftus! They're using incendiary bombs!'

'Don't talk in exclamation marks,' said Loftus irritably. 'I fancied they were. Where?'

'At the side entrance.'

'Have you been to the front?'

'Yes, it's all quiet there. But what are we going to do?'

'What can we do?' asked Loftus. 'Try to put the fires out, and hope to God that someone gets along in time. We can't go out.'

'Someone must get word through to Winchester,' muttered Mayhew. 'The water comes from a well, and it's been blocked up. We've no means of putting out the fire, and it will be blazing everywhere in half an hour.'

'Ye-es,' said Loftus. 'All the same, we can't get out.'

'We can try,' said Mayhew grimly.

Loftus rested a hand on his shoulder.

'Mayhew, I agree with you in principle. But we've got to try parleying with the gentlemen outside. If we try to get through for help, we'll just be mown down.'

'In the dark...'

'It's not dark to them,' said Loftus quietly.

'Don't be a damned fool!' snapped Mayhew.

'*Loftus!*'

The call came from some way off, but it was comparatively loud and spoken so oddly that Mayhew broke off in the middle of his sentence. The voice, thought Loftus, was coming through a megaphone, and probably from the direction of the front door. He did not recognise it, but the 's' had a sibilance that reminded him of Oundle's description of Forster's hissing utterance.

'Loftus!'

As the second call came Oundle came hurrying from the main hall. He was smoke-grimed and dishevelled, and his big eyes were no longer ingenuous.

'A gent outside wants a word with you, Bill.'

'I heard,' said Loftus. 'Where is he?'

'Somewhere near the front door. If we had a stick of dynamite, we might do some damage.'

'If you had a mind you might do some thinking,' retorted Loftus with acerbity. He led the way towards the hall, and as he reached it the Cartwrights came down the stairs. Several of the clerical staff of that evacuated department were standing by, scared but controlling themselves well. From somewhere upstairs came a hysterical crying, probably from a maid.

Cartwright's ascetic face was pale and tight-lipped.

'Loftus, there's to be no bargaining with him.'

'No?' asked Loftus. 'I...'

For the third time—*'Loftus!'* came the cry.

Loftus stepped forward towards the barricaded front door, and the light shone vividly down on him. As he reached the settee which had been upturned he vaulted lightly so that he perched himself on top of the barricade, and peered into the semi-darkness beyond. As though idly, he put on his glasses.

The semi-darkness took on that bluish tinge, while he could see everything crystal celar. There was a Lagonda drawn up outside the front door, while on a tripod beside it was a

Lewis gun. No men were in sight and on their feet, but two were stretched out, motionless.

'Speaking,' called Loftus.

Forster's voice came from the car, but Loftus doubted whether the man was in it. Probably he was speaking from some distance off, and the words were relayed by loud-speaker.

'It's time you came,' called Forster, and, behind Loftus, Mayhew, Oundle and Thornton listened tensely. 'I don't mean to waste words. I can see as well as you can in daylight, and no man or woman comes out of the place alive until I say so. Fire has started in three places, and you've no water to put it out. Do you understand that?'

'Perfectly,' said Loftus, and he still seemed unconcerned.

'You don't seem to.' The man spoke so colloquially that he might have been English, but for the sibilance of his 's'. 'You can go, and the others—except the Cartwrights. Send them out—that's all I want from you this time.'

'Oh,' said Loftus. 'You want the Cartwrights in exchange for our safety, is that it?'

'And what Cartwright is carrying,' said Forster.

'H'mm. It might be possible,' said Loftus. 'I'll ask them. What happens if you don't get what you want?'

'We wait until the place is gutted.'

'While it gets gutted people will come,' said Loftus, 'and when it's gutted everything you want goes with it. Wouldn't you call that short-sighted?'

'Don't imagine that I'm not serious,' said Forster. 'If I don't get the thing, no one else will. And I'll get Grafton, he'll find it sooner or later. If you don't send those two out, you're finished. All of you. Understand?'

'I'll call you again in five minutes,' said Loftus.

He did not wait for an answer, but jumped down.

Mayhew was looking bewilderedly at him. Oundle and Thornton were eyeing the Cartwrights, and James Cartwright was standing quite still, with his hands clenched at his side. Garry was smoking a cigarette, and except for Loftus she seemed the most unconcerned there.

'He's very definite,' said Loftus. 'I—Mayhew, you might get the hall cleared.'

Mayhew hesitated, and then obeyed. All of his men were with him now, and the half-dozen members of the staff were ushered into the billiards-room, which was as safe as anywhere in the house. As they went it was possible to hear the increasing roar of flames. Loftus knew that the three fires were rapidly gaining a hold, and he knew that the lull in the battle could not last for long.

Mayhew turned back from the billiards-room door.

'Now then, what is all this? What's Cartwright got that the madman outside wants?'

'A moment,' said Loftus. 'Put the lights out, Ned...' He waited until darkness descended, darkness broken only by the faint flicker from the fire in the kitchen quarters. Then he put the glasses on Mayhew's face.

'Good—*God!*'

'Excusable,' said Loftus dryly. 'Cartwright has the secret of that, and Nazi Forster wants it. Do you subscribe to letting Forster have the Cartwrights?'

'God!' repeated Mayhew, and as the lights were switched on again he looked startled out of his life. 'No, a thousand times no! But we've got to get help. I...'

A man came running down the stairs, voices were raised on the first landing. Loftus stopped the man as he reached the hall.

'What is it?'

'We—we can't—stay up there.' It was one of the clerical

staff who had been sent round to block the windows. 'There's a fire on the second floor, three rooms are blazing. Get us out of here for God's sake!'

'What are the others doing?'

'Trying to stop it.'

'Nice work,' said Loftus. 'Mayhew, there's your job. Organise three parties, and have each party attack one of the fires. Cartwright, you're all right for the time being, we don't propose giving you away.'

Cartwright said: 'That's as well.'

'And there isn't time for argument,' snapped Loftus.

'There's time for this,' said Mayhew, and his voice was steadier than it had been a minute before. 'I'm going to try to get through. I want a volunteer from one of you...' He stared at the three uniformed policemen, and one of them stepped forward promptly, the others after only a moment's thought. 'All right, Meeson, you can come.'

'Don't be a damned fool,' said Loftus. 'There isn't a chance at the moment.'

'We've got to try,' said Mayhew. 'You're doing a hell of a lot of talk, but nothing else. We'll start from the morning-room window, Meeson. Keep low, and once we're outside we separate.'

Loftus gripped his arm.

'Leave it to me, will you? There's one way of getting through this, but you haven't found it. I...'

Mayhew wrenched his arm away. He was a burly specimen, and he could use his fists. He used them then, on Loftus. The punch took Loftus in the stomach, and doubled him up— and at the same time a gun flashed into the inspector's hand.

'Stop anyone moving.' He handed the gun to one of the other policemen. 'Take this.'

The man obeyed.

Oundle and Thornton hesitated, not sure whether to try to reach the morning-room first. They were not carrying their guns in sight, and the burly policeman looked as if he would shoot if there was a single movement.

Mayhew and Meeson went into the morning-room. There was a short pause, and then the squeaking of a window. Another pause, and a whisper:

'All right—come on.'

Mayhew's voice, and it suggested that he was outside. There was a moment's hesitation, and then a smothered curse, as if Meeson had banged his knee climbing out of the window. Silence: and then:

Tap-tap-tap-tap-tap.

'Oh, my God!' muttered Thornton.

Loftus straightened up, his face pale, his stomach uneasy.

'Poor devils,' he muttered. He looked at the other policeman, and Oundle spoke for him.

'Still think that's the way to try and make it?'

'No, sir.' The Robert with the gun was staring towards the morning-room door, and he took a step forward. Oundle pushed his way ahead, going through first. Loftus rested for a moment against the wall, with the Cartwrights and Thornton the only others in sight since Oundle and the two policemen had gone into the morning-room. Oundle had switched on the lights.

Oundle could see Mayhew and Meeson stretched out on the ground not two yards from the window. Both men were riddled with bullets, which had caught their faces.

Garry Cartwright said: 'Loftus, *is* there a way out?'

'What was that about gas?' asked Loftus.

'Useless here,' said Cartwright abruptly. 'I've only a couple of grenades, and there's too much wind for them to be used effectively.'

'What is it?'

'Chlorine.'

'Nice fellow,' said Loftus. 'I...'

Crash!

They did not know what it was, but it crashed against the stairs and exploded—but not with a detonation loud or forceful enough to make them lose their balance. There was a second, and a third, and Loftus roared:

'Gas grenades! Get out—get out of the hall!'

He grabbed Garry Cartwright and moved for the billiards-room, but fast though he went he was too late. Something clutched his throat—something potent but unseen, making him gasp and splutter, bringing tears to his eyes, a furious burning to his nose and mouth. He staggered, and then pitched forward—and one after the other the gathering in the hall went down before the gas which Forster had used while Loftus and Cartwright had been thinking it out.

The gas worked in the house, even though it would be useless outside.

There was a moment of silence, but for the burning that was coming from the domestic quarters and from the second landing. And then a man vaulted over the front-door barricade. A short, thick-set man wearing a military gas-mask.

A second—a third—a fourth.

They hurried towards the outstretched figures on the hall carpet, and they did not waste time. Two of them lifted Cartwright, and the third raised his sister as easily as if she were a feather-weight. They went back, making no effort to injure Loftus or the others.

Forster, also wearing a mask, met them outside.

'You've got them both?'

'Yes, sir.'

'Ex-cellent,' said Forster very softly. 'Excellent indeed. Now fire the hall.'

And as he spoke a man at his side tossed a small grenade into the hall—a bomb which burst with a deafening explosion, and then spread liquid fire all about it. A second, a third. The fire ran slowly about the carpet, smoke billowed through the doorway, while Forster and his men and their prisoners made for their cars.

Loftus and the others remained unconscious.

14
SAYS MARK

H ere it is,' said Mark Errol. 'They've turned off the road. I... Gosh, Wally. Something's burning.'

'I wouldn't be surprised,' drawled Mr. Wallace Davidson.

It was Davidson who had crashed his car when trying to help Oundle earlier in the day, Davidson who had afterwards located Mark Errol, and had been at the Cliff Royal Hotel when Forster—presumably—had attacked, using gas and getting away without difficulty and with the person of Professor Grafton. Davidson who had recovered first and telephoned Craigie, and Davidson who had been told that Craigie had tried to telephone Grayling Manor without success.

'Get there quickly,' Craigie had said. 'I'm warning the local police to stand by in case of need, but look round first. If there's no sign of Loftus, or any suggestion of trouble, get the local men busy at once.'

And now the police patrol car which had led Davidson and Mark Errol to the Manor swung off the road into the drive. Ahead of them they saw the flames which were coming from the first-floor windows. The police car ahead pulled up, and Mark Errol jammed on his brakes.

A peak-capped policeman came up at the same time.

'Fire ahead, sir, and...'

'Cut back to the nearest telephone,' said Wally. 'Have the fire-brigade from Winchester, and tell Police Headquarters that the warning from London takes effect. Understood?'

'Yes, sir. You'd better get past us.'

'Right,' said Davidson.

But he waited long enough to lean over the headlamps, and wrench off the covers. The brilliant lights that shot out were strictly against regulations, but they showed the trees, skeletons without their leaves, the shrubs and the banks on either side of the drive. Farther ahead they seemed to shine on men moving between the trees.

And as Mark backed the Talbot he was driving, to get past the patrol car, there came the loud reports of three separate explosions.

There was no longer the slightest doubt about the shadows being men, while a machine-gun opened fire without a second's warning. The police car had backed towards the gates, and Mark trod on the accelerator of the Talbot.

Bullets rattled against the sides but rebounded, for the car was armoured. Both men crouched low; both were worried far more than they were ever likely to say by the possible fate of Loftus and the others.

Men were moving about on all sides.

The machine-gunning stopped, although now and again a revolver shot rang out, and it was not safe for them to raise their heads. The drive seemed never ending, although as they drew nearer to the house they could see the flames more clearly—and the Lagonda with several men nearby.

Other cars were hidden along the drive.

One after the other they started off, but Davidson and Errol paid no heed to them. Their one concern was to get to the house. They were able to look ahead, and in the blazing headlights of their car they saw two men carrying another—and one man with a body flung fireman fashion over his shoulder.

'Business,' said Davidson, and used his gun.

His bullet brought the man down, while whatever he was carrying thudded to the ground. The Lagonda's engine started, and as it passed the Talbot Errol swung the wheel to the left to avoid a collision. Davidson saw the masked figures inside. Even had there been a chance of crashing the car he would not have taken it. Someone inside might be a prisoner.

Flames were leaping from the front door.

The headlights were lost in the glow, now, while the noise of burning and occasionally the crashing of furniture inside was deafening. Smuts and smoke were all about them, and it was difficult to breathe.

'Respirators,' called Errol.

Both men carried the service type, and both fitted them as they hurried towards the porch. The barricade offered an obstacle far more difficult to surmount now than it had done earlier in the evening, for the wood was scorching.

Davidson made the jump.

He touched the top of the sideboard, staggered in mid-air, but steadied himself as he reached the hall. Mark Errol scrambled after him, and they saw the leaping flames, with the whole of one wall ablaze, and a part of the parquet flooring charred and red-hot.

They also saw Loftus, Oundle and Thornton and two policemen, near an open door—and others whom they did not recognise. As they hurried towards Loftus, the soles of whose shoes were actually curling, and likely to catch fire at any moment—they saw the greenish tinge on the faces of the men.

'I'll lug these out,' Wally said. 'Look around.'

Errol started off, and by chance reached the billiards-room first. As he burst in, a dozen startled men stared anxiously. They had been brought back from the cellar. All of them knew that the place was on fire—but none of them knew what had happened to the men in the hall.

Errol banged the door to, and took off his mask.

'Outside, all of you—that window there.'

A man shouted.

'But we can't, the guns...'

'They've gone. You've been rescued,' said Mark Errol, and grinned. 'Anyone else about?'

'On the first and second floor,' said a sturdy youngster who seemed to have himself in hand more than any of the others.

'All right. I'll fetch 'em. Keep out of the hall.'

'Why?'

'Gas,' said Errol.

He readjusted his mask and went back into the hall. Wally was dragging a policeman into the morning-room, which had so far escaped from the flames, but the heat was increasing, and he had stripped off coat and waistcoat. Errol hurried up the stairs, and on the first landing saw five men, all stretched out.

Each had a greenish tinge on his face.

'Gosh!' exclaimed Mark Errol, and for a split second he paused.

Then he carried one man downstairs, and then a second.

Wally joined in. They were sweating, and beneath the masks their faces were beaded in perspiration. Most of the time they worked blindly, sweat in their eyes and smeared across the goggles of the masks.

Then, abruptly, there came the clanging of a fire-engine bell. A second, a third. Through the morning-room window three steel-helmeted A.F.S. men burst, and they did not need telling what to do.

Davidson stretched up, and leaned for a moment against the wall.

'That,' he said, 'is that. I could do with a drink.'

There was little chance of saving the building. The place was searched as thoroughly as it could be for men, but no more were found. Some filing cabinets and three or four safes were brought from the main offices, but most of the papers there went up in smoke.

Every fire-engine for miles around came, and pipes were laid to a stream which went through the outlying grounds. A.F.S. men and regulars played their part, while the lurid glare made mockery of the black-out, and was seen as far away as Winchester and Basingstoke and the villages around.

Davidson and Errol visited Winchester Hospital. Loftus, Oundle, Thornton and the others who had been gassed were there under treatment—together with a girl who had been picked up by the rescue squads just outside the front door of the Manor. Near her had been a man shot through the knee— and Davidson remembered the shooting, realised when he was told where the girl had been found that he had prevented her from joining the men in the Lagonda.

'She won't be sorry,' Errol opined.

Both men were washed, and refreshed, and their thirsts were slaked. But their eyes were red-rimmed, and they still showed traces of that desperate fight against time.

A short, dapper man came out of a room near the passage

in which they were waiting, and Davidson asked with as little concern as he could contrive:

'How are the gas-patients, Doctor?'

'We-ell.' The little man frowned. 'One or two are doubtful, I'm afraid, very doubtful. Others will be all right quite quickly. There is a chlorine constituent in the gas, but something else which I haven't yet been able to identify. It is the first time I have handled gas cases except experimental ones, which are never, of course, quite the same. In the event of the distribution of poison gases from the air, such experience will be invaluable. It...'

'A very big, tall man,' said Errol softly. 'How is he?'

'Oh, doing quite well. I...' The doctor peered at them shortsightedly, and seemed perturbed. 'Aren't you police officers?'

'No,' said Wally. 'We're friends of the patients.'

'I'm dreadfully sorry!' The little man was obviously sincere. 'If you'd care to see them—quiet, please.'

There was Loftus, Thornton and Oundle, two policemen and the others from the clerical staff, stretched out on small beds in a ward which had been hurriedly cleared to take the gas cases. Loftus's bed seemed absurdly small, and his head was touching the black-enamelled head panel. He was breathing easily, and he seemed to have regained his normal colour.

At the far end of the ward there was a screen round one bed; by another bed there were two nurses.

'How long before they're able to talk?' Wally asked, huskily.

'A day or two, at the most,' the doctor said. 'Perhaps a few hours.'

'Thanks,' said Wally. 'And, Doctor—be as careful with them as you would be with a Cabinet Minister.'

'Or a farm-labourer,' said the dapper little man. 'You need have no fears, gentlemen.'

They felt greatly reassured.

* * *

Gordon Craigie had sent word that he was coming to Winchester, and that they were to wait for him there. Normally he would have reached the Hampshire city an hour before the other two had visited the hospital. But as he had left Whitehall, and reached Parliament Street, a breathless constable had loomed up in the darkness.

That had been about half-past nine.

'Excuse me, sir...'

'Hallo, Mulliner, what it it?'

They've been trying to get you on the phone, sir.'

'They', to Mulliner, meant the Prime Minister. The Rt. Hon. David Wishart, a considerate man, was popular with those policemen who guarded the door of No. 10, and those detectives whose duty it was to follow him. Secretly he disliked it, but even before the war he had been compelled to accept it. There had been attacks on the lives of several Cabinet Ministers, and Wishart was considered too vital to the country's needs to allow the slightest risk of assassination.

Mulliner was one of the most familiar figures in that part of Whitehall. Tall and bulky, never likely to rise above a sergeant's pay—if he ever reached it—he was stolid and dependable, an ox of a man, some said, but with shrewd kindliness and devotion to duty.

Breathing hard, he walked alongside Craigie.

'Glad I caught you, sir.'

'Did Mr. Wishart send you *to* the office?' Craigie asked, for he knew that only in an emergency would Wishart send Mulliner—or anyone—to the office in Whitehall.

'Yessir.'

That did not sound promising.

Craigie tapped on the door of Number 10, and was admitted by a footman who knew him well. It was a homely household; it was difficult to believe the great decisions which had been taken in its comparatively small rooms.

Wishart, tall, grey-haired, tired-looking and lined of face, was standing with his back to the fire. Opposite him was Jonathan Scott, Foreign Minister under the Wishart War Government, and in the Cabinet probably the most unpopular member; he had a disconcerting way of saying precisely what he thought. The other members of the War Cabinet felt that his language, particularly from a man who controlled the most delicate of tasks, was reprehensible. Nor could they understand Wishart's faith in Scott, who certainly had enemies in foreign capitals.

It was even said that Scott could have persuaded Wishart to have made further concessions to the Nazi Government, and thus avoided the war. In more bated breath it was said that Scott had *wanted* the war.

And he was one of the three members of the Cabinet with whom Gordon Craigie had much patience. Wishart was the second, and Lawrence, the recently appointed First Lord, was the third.

Lawrence was also present.

He was a burly looking man, with a chunky face, and a cigar sticking from the corner of loose lips which could give forth the fires of oratory. His eyes were hooded, but beneath their lids very bright, very shrewd. He, like Scott, spoke his mind and knew unpopularity.

'So he caught you,' said Wishart. 'I'm glad, Craigie. I needed a word with you quickly. Just what is happening on your front?'

Wishart, decided Craigie, was wool-gathering—which

meant that something unexpected and perhaps disastrous had developed. Wishart was always inclined to dither when he first had bad news, but the stage was a temporary one.

He had dithered when Russia had marched into Poland and there were people who considered that he should have looked on Russia as an aggressor as much as Germany. He had wilted for half an hour when the first big troop-carrying liner had been sunk by U-boat action. He had seemed to wilt under the onslaught of the magnetic mines—and yet he always gathered himself together quickly, and proved himself to be capable, quick-thinking, and positive in what he did.

Scott and Lawrence were different types. It was Scott who asked sharply:

'You've heard nothing, Craigie?'

'About what?'

'The *Ibrox* has been sunk by enemy action, *after dark*.'

Scott emphasised the last two words, and then looked at the Chief of Department Z. Lawrence cleared his throat.

'No doubt that she was seen, Craigie.'

'We had hoped,' said Wishart abruptly, 'that this invention was only in its early stages, but...' He shrugged, and his voice grew more brisk. 'Craigie, we must have a full report from you quickly. Has any progress been made?'

Craigie said slowly: 'A little, but not much. I'm going down to find out what has been happening at Grayling now.'

'Yes, yes,' said Scott testily. He was a man with a great regard for Gordon Craigie—but he had never known Craigie in action during war-time. 'A bad business down there, but it's not of vital importance. This see-in-the-dark matter...'

'The man who claims to hold the secret was at Grayling Manor this evening,' said Craigie mildly. 'Or near there. Loftus came through...'

He spoke quietly, giving them the gist of Loftus's report,

and contriving in few words to give a résumé of the Department's activity during the past three days. He did not once raise his voice, and he kept one hand in his pocket.

He finished: 'Consequently I must find out what has happened at Grayling. Loftus and others have been gassed, but there seems to be some hope that they'll be able to talk before the night is out. In any case, a woman down there might be able to give us valuable information.'

Scott laughed, a deep, barking sound.

'Good enough. Sorry, Craigie; I thought you were out of your depth.'

Lawrence smiled crookedly.

'But let's be frank, Craigie—you haven't got far yet.'

Craigie shrugged. 'It took you some time to find the *Graf Spee*. We've had just under three days so far, and started from scratch.'

'We have every faith in you, Craigie,' said Wishart, and Craigie knew that the period of uncertainty had gone. 'We must counteract this thing, Craigie. You understand the implications of the *Ibrox*, of course?'

'My dear sir, yes. But she was sunk at long range, I take it?'

'Five or six miles.' said Lawrence. '*In the dark.*' He tossed the end of his cigar into the fire, and bit off the end of another. All four men were silent, brooding over the implications: there was a weapon which meant that warfare, on land and sea and air, could be waged as effectively at night as by day.

And the Nazis had it—or appeared to have it.

'Well...' Wishart straightened his shoulders. 'You'll get down to Grayling, Craigie. Telephone me, will you?'

'Yes.'

'Luck,' said Lawrence, briefly.

Scott accompanied Craigie to the door, and they parted outside, Scott walking towards St. James's Park and Craigie towards Whitehall. It was Scott who saw P.C. Mulliner loom out of the darkness and flash a torch in his face.

'All right, Mulliner—good night.'

'Good night, sir. Oh, pardon me, but...'

Odd words, from Mulliner. Scott fancied that the constable was under the stress of some emotion, and stopped and faced the man. The man he thought was Mulliner—hit him powerfully in the stomach. Scott gasped and doubled up, and the man in P.C. Mulliner's clothes, and who looked very like that trusted policeman, cracked a right to the chin, which knocked the Foreign Minister completely out.

Two shroudy figures joined him, while a car drove up silently and Scott was bundled in.

15

THE HUSH-HUSH DEPARTMENT

Craigie was unaware of the disappearance of Jonathan Scott. He sped towards Winchester with a Special Service car ahead of him, and another behind.

The lights of the three cars were more powerful than those used by the average motorist, and Craigie made the run in a little more than two hours. Stiff with driving, he stepped into the police station just after midnight, to find Wally Davidson and Mark Errol in two arm-chairs of Victorian style but obviously comfortable, in the charge-room. A sergeant on duty was at his desk, perched on a stool.

Craigie coughed.

The sergeant looked up, and Davidson opened one eye. Slowly he uncoiled his long frame from the chair, while Errol began to stir.

'Hallo,' said Davidson. 'We thought you'd been gassed too.'

'Is Loftus conscious?' asked Craigie.

'He wasn't half an hour ago,' said Davidson.

'Is he still at the hospital?'

'Yes.'

'Let's get there,' said Craigie.

Davidson drove him there.

He was more worried than he had been before, for Loftus's continued unconsciousness suggested that his chief agent would be *hors de combat* for some time.

There was no one to replace Loftus.

Most of the men would do their part and none of them were fools. But they lacked that little something which Loftus possessed to a degree almost as great as Craigie. He could organise quickly, he was ruthless; if he acted slowly—as he had at the Manor that evening—there was always a reason for it. The men, in their way, worshipped him. Not one member of the Department would hesitate for a split-second to obey a command from Loftus, even though it appeared to mean certain death.

Craigie was shown into the ward by a disapproving matron—and as Craigie entered, Loftus stirred and opened his eyes. He did not show any immediate sign of recognition. Craigie's heart leapt.

The night doctor, a big man, nodded brusquely.

'Good evening, sir. Mr. Carter?'

'Yes,' said Craigie: he was 'Carter' whenever he was on official business but did not want his real name known. 'You've been told by telephone of the importance of this, Doctor. How is Mr. Loftus?'

'He should be able to talk within an hour,' said the medico. 'There was a little chlorine in the gas, but an admixture of a chloroform vapour which brought unconsciousness but was unlikely to cause death. Only one man appears to be in danger of losing his life.'

Craigie nodded more brusquely than he intended.

'Thanks. Will you arrange for Mr. Loftus to have a private ward, and...'

138

'Also the lady,' said William Loftus.

It was more of a croak than an ordinary speaking voice, and his expression did not change. He seemed to be staring blankly at Craigie, and for a moment the Chief felt alarm. Then:

'Can anyone,' went on Loftus in the same harsh voice, 'advise something for a thick head?'

Craigie laughed, which he had not expected to do again that night.

'I'll get you something,' said the doctor quickly.

'For the love of Mike do. Gordon—don't forget that girl, she's important. Mark's lady-love. And don't expect another word from me until my head stops hammering.'

Actually it continued to hammer when, two hours later, Loftus sat up in a bed which was a little nearer the size that he needed. He had been able to keep down weak bouillon and was feeling well enough but for the head which threatened to lift itself from his shoulders of its own volition.

He talked...

Craigie, Davidson and Mark Errol listened.

Oundle and Thornton were in a private ward. Spats had taken the gas badly, and was likely to be out of action for some weeks. Oundle would be up within a couple of days.

'And that's all I can tell you,' Loftus said. 'Summarised: First, the man Forster...'

'Look at this,' said Wally.

He had been writing as Loftus had talked, for he was a man with an orderly mind, and he liked to get things in black and white when he could. Loftus glanced down a list which ran:

(a) Forster, Nazi or free-lance spy, has:

(b) A supply of the specially fitted glass, Cartwright—who presumably has the formula for the lens and

(c) A body of men of unknown strength prepared to use any kind of lethal weapon.

(d) Presumably he has Grafton, who he believes can work on the formula to bring about the lens.

(e) We have Cartwright's sister, who seems to know a great deal, some of the glasses, and an idea of the power of them.

'First class,' said Loftus. 'Even to the "presumably he has Grafton". We took that for granted, but he distinctly said, "I'll get Grafton", which suggests the kidnappers at Bournemouth were not Forster's men.' He grinned crookedly, for his lips were swollen, and any movement of his face was painful. 'Is that all, Gordon?'

Loftus of course knew that it wasn't. Craigie's manner was proof of the fact that there was more trouble than had yet been admitted.

'It's not, Bill,' Craigie said. 'This lens gives visibility at a distance of six or seven miles. We've proof of it.'

'My God!' said Loftus simply.

'Seven *miles*,' breathed Davidson, and for once he did not look weary.

'Who's got it?' rasped Mark Errol.

Craigie said slowly:

'We lost a destroyer tonight, after dark by long-range gunfire. So Berlin has it, and yet...'

'A minute,' Loftus said, and already he felt more clear-headed. 'If Berlin's got it, Forster can't be working for them.'

'It appears that way,' admitted Craigie.

'He told me, in effect, that he was.'

'No one else would sink a destroyer of ours,' said Errol.

'I wouldn't say that.' Loftus hitched himself up in bed, and stared at Craigie. 'The Russians might, conceivably. Other countries aren't as friendly towards us as they might be. But there's another thing.'

He hesitated for a moment and the others waited without interruption. Then went on in a voice which seemed to come from a long way off:

'Gordon, if you'd heard Cartwright you would know what I was driving at. Cartwright struck me as being a good fellow with an obsession against Government officials, this Government's officials in particular. Not the type to do anything like the Hundred-and-One crowd[1], but a genuine internationalist convinced we're doing everything the wrong way round. He is confident that he could beat us, and gave me the impression that he was a lot stronger than we realised.'

Craigie frowned.

'How do you mean?'

'I don't know. But no man in his senses—and he's sane enough even if he's got a bee in his bonnet about this—would expect to be able to exert pressure on the Government with nothing more than a small gang of men behind him. Cartwright had something up his sleeve, but didn't have the chance to say what. He made threats, but vague ones. Now...' Loftus lifted his hands, palm upwards. 'What I'm getting at is this: Cartwright is the man who holds the secret of this lens. There can't be any reasonable doubt of that.'

'Well?' said Craigie.

'He *could* have a warship or two,' said Loftus.

'My dear man!' drawled Wally, 'you were gassed, I know, but...'

'Hold it,' said Errol. 'What size guns are needed to sink a destroyer?'

'Four-inch should do it,' said Craigie.

'Any semi-armoured ship can carry four-inch guns, or even six-inch,' said Mark Errol. 'Anyone can buy guns. I'm beginning to think Bill's got it.'

'Thank you,' said Loftus dryly. 'Ring for some tea, Wally, do something useful if you can't contribute a little common sense. Cartwright knew that he had this thing, and he's the type to demonstrate this way.'

Craigie frowned, while a nurse entered, and Wally asked her amiably if she would bring some very weak tea for a very weak patient. This was typical of the Department men; they could keep a level balance only by that exaggerated facetiousness.

'What time did the destroyer go down?' Loftus asked when the nurse had gone.

'Some time before eight this evening.'

'And it was about eight that we were in the middle of my shindy,' said Loftus. He frowned, looking up towards the ceiling, while the others kept still. 'There's just one thing.'

'What is it?'

'Cartwright might be one of a bunch.'

'Ye-es,' said Craigie, and he looked at his watch. 'I wonder how long it will be before his sister can talk?'

'It might be a long, long time,' said Loftus. 'She struck me as being as cool as ice and harder than granite. I wish Diana were here.'

Diana Woodward, Loftus's fiancée and also in the service of Department Z—whither she had come by way of the American Secret Intelligence Department some two years before—was in the States. She was combining routine work for Craigie with a personal round of visits, and she would have been in England a fortnight before but for the sudden increase of attacks on neutral shipping, and the consequent belatedness of all cross-Atlantic sailings. Diana, Loftus believed, would be able to handle Garry Cartwright more effectively than any man.

She would have to be handled, and the job would be his.

'I'll go and see her,' Craigie said.

'I'm going to get up,' said Loftus.

Tea arrived as he spoke, and the nurse who brought it immediately reported to the doctor. In the middle of tea and thoughts that were a long way from pleasant, Bill Loftus was visited by a grim-faced and dour medico, who told him that he must stay in bed for another twenty-four hours, or take the consequences.

'Which would be?' asked Loftus amiably.

'You might collapse, and if you do it will be a long job.'

'I don't feel a bit like collapsing,' said Loftus, and when he saw the glint of anger in the medico's eyes he smiled in a way which few people could resist. 'Sorry, Doc, but the matter's urgent. You've made a pretty good job of me, and I've got to take a chance with the rest.'

The medico shrugged.

'It's your own life,' he said.

'That's just the trouble,' said Loftus. 'It isn't, at the moment. Have my clothes sent in, and then slip along to the lady's ward, will you? Mr. Carter's there now.'

'She's as well and as obstinate as you,' said the doctor with a shrug.

Craigie was gone for nearly half an hour, which did not surprise them. Loftus used the time in learning details of the attack on the Cliff Royal. It had been so sudden that there had been little or no chance of fighting back; the gas which had been used had had less effect than that used at the Manor, however; both Davidson and Errol had been dosed, but there had been no ill-effects.

'Another hint that it wasn't Forster, or the gas would have been the same,' said Loftus. 'What about the man Grey?'

'He was out, too.'

'Did he recover?'

'He was a bit talkative afterwards,' said Errol, 'and he's heard something about Warncliffe.'

'Ye-es,' said Craigie. 'A queer angle, the Warncliffe-cum-Janice Grafton one. Someone is looking after them, of course.'

'Yes. Although looking after doesn't get us far in this business,' said Mike Errol. 'They seem to know just where we are all the time, light or dark.'

Loftus shrugged, and adjusted his tie.

'It's the whole trouble, my Mark. Eyes in the dark. A very useful thing. My God, it can break us if Germany gets away with it. *Break* us.'

Each man knew that it was true.

Not one of them had ever blinded themselves to the likelihood of a long war. They knew that Germany, half-starved though many of its people might be, and facing internal difficulties far worse than were ever likely to come in England, was prepared for a struggle that would last for years. Talk of a crack-up from the inside was to a degree reassuring, but the Department knew that in most cases the wish was father to the thought. Economically Germany was unsound—but force could get what money could not. The neutrals were forced into making concessions and supplying goods, which they did for England on a strictly cash basis. Most sections of the German people had been convinced that the war was necessary, that the Allies were in truth the aggressors, and they would tighten their belts and fight. The comparatively small People's Front was courageous and tenacious—but its broadcasts had more effect outside of Germany than in it.

Loftus did not pretend that he thought the war would be over quickly. Success depended, as with the British it always would, on the control of the high seas.

At the moment that control was in Allied hands.

The submarine menace had been reduced to a negligible

quantity; magnetic mines had flared into prominence, but soon died down. The attacks on neutral shipping were on the increase, but were having no direct effect on the war, while supplies were reaching England regularly and in ample quantities. The pocket battleships, virtual pirates in the Atlantic, had been hemmed into neutral harbours and interned, or had been sent to the bottom. Since Lawrence had taken over at the Admiralty, Germany had been swept virtually from the seas.

But now this weapon brought a greater, deeper menace than ever before.

Death and destruction, by night.

By land, sea, or air.

And one ship had gone, others might be reported at any moment. The effect of the weapon on the Allied cause could be disastrous. In a matter of weeks, if not in days, the ascendancy which the Allies had gained could be swept away. There had been no decisive action yet; with this weapon the side which possessed it *must* be the victor in the first major encounter.

At best the lens would prolong the war indefinitely.

At worst it could lose it for the Allies.

Loftus said slowly:

'Well, we know where we are. And if Garry Cartwright is going to be awkward, we'll have to change her mind. Not a nice thought,' he added bleakly.

Errol grunted: 'No.'

That was the first intimation that Bill Loftus had received that Mark Errol remembered the Waterloo encounter with anything more than self-reproach. He eyed the man quickly— and he saw enough to know that the brief meeting had meant something to Mark.

Loftus, who often told his lady that he had fallen in love with her photograph in a matter of seconds, did not pass the matter over too lightly. Mark, glancing at him, saw something of what was in the other's mind. He shrugged.

'It'll pass.'

'Take it easy,' said Loftus. 'Well, I'm going to see Craigie.'

But he did not get as far as the girl's ward.

Craigie was coming along the passage towards him, and it was one of those rare occasions when Craigie really betrayed that he was worried. His eyes were opened wider than usual, and his face looked gaunt. He gripped Loftus's arm, and Loftus felt the sharp pressure of his thin fingers.

Loftus's heart sank.

'God! She's not dead? Or missing?'

'No,' said Craigie. 'She's coming round all right. Bill, this is more serious than anything yet. Jonathan Scott has been kidnapped.'

'*What?*'

'The Foreign Minister, *kidnapped*,' repeated Craigie, and he continued to stare blankly at Bill Loftus. 'Someone phoned the information to his wife, and she called Wishart. He was taken from Downing Street. The policeman on duty there, named Mulliner, was found dead in St. James's Park; obviously he had been impersonated. We—we must get him back. The question is, who took him? Forster's people, or the Cartwrights?'

'I think,' said Loftus grimly, 'that I'd better have a word with the girl.'

---

1. See *Panic* by John Creasey.

16
RE-ENTER WARNCLIFFE

She was dressed, and sitting in an easy-chair, next to the bed in the private ward to which she had been taken. But for the patches beneath her eyes, in a dark suit, she looked well. She was as cool as she had ever been, and the cigarette was dangling from her lips—as inevitable, it seemed, as Craigie's meerschaum or Lawrence's cigar.

Outside her door were two policemen.

Outside the window were two others.

She had been told that, and she had no gun, no weapon at all that she might use, even had she thought of trying to escape. She looked up at Loftus with one brow raised a little above the other.

'So you're on your feet?'

'I am, my dear,' said Loftus gently. 'And I'm particularly glad to see that you are. I hope you're not as obstinate as your brother.'

'It depends what it's about,' said Garry Cartwright. 'What part of the world have you taken him to? Dartmoor? Or Cannon Row?'

Loftus sat on the end of the bed.

'Forster got him,' he announced bluntly.

She leaned forward in her chair, gripping the arms until her knuckles showed white. He saw the tension which had come to her face, the horror in her eyes.

'God, no, anyone but *Forster*!'

'But for a lucky break, he would have had you,' said Loftus. 'There was a lot too much fooling at the Manor, and he lost out. We had all the luck in the world—you did in particular. Whom do you work with?' he added abruptly.

'Friends.'

'Could they give instructions apart from him?'

'I wonder,' said Garry Cartwright, and her eyes were normal now.

Loftus said in a softer voice:

'How many ships have you fitted with guns?'

Again her eyes widened, her hands clenched, and she actually half-rose to her feet. Half-standing, half-sitting, she stared up into a face which no longer seemed good-humoured: and she said in a voice he could hardly hear:

'What—do you mean?'

'Precisely that,' said Loftus. 'A ship has been sunk.'

'By—night?' She whispered the word.

'By night.'

'Oh, God!' she said, and said again: 'Oh, God! They've gone mad, they must have done! They weren't to use that unless we had real trouble with you, and I didn't think we would. It...'

And then she stopped, and her shoulders straightened.

'I'm sorry, Loftus. Questions won't help you.'

'I see,' said Loftus. He turned to the door, and pressed a bell close to it. When a nurse tapped, he called: 'Send the two younger gentlemen from my ward in, please, with a tray of surgical instruments.'

'What, sir?'

'Do it quickly,' snapped Loftus, and he won a gasp as the nurse turned away. He looked at Garry Cartwright, and he saw incredulity in her eyes—but she was breathing more quickly.

'What—are you going to do?' she asked.

'You should know,' he said casually. 'I'm going to find out what you know, if after causing you a lot of pain or not. I've done it before, but not with a woman. You don't know what pain a scalpel can cause, do you? And...'

'You wouldn't dare!'

'And now she gets all dramatic,' said Loftus, and he grinned. 'I may seem to be fooling, but I'm not. I...' He stepped forward suddenly, gripped her wrists and crushed them together in his great hand. He half-lifted her, by her wrists, from the chair. And then he let her fall back, and he went on in a dead voice:

'Understand this. Over a hundred lives were lost tonight in a demonstration of this thing which you and your brother have found. They were drowned—understand? Some of them battered almost to pieces before the ship went down. Others were crushed and trapped so that they had no chance to get away. It looked like a Nazi action, and that would have been war. It was your friends, and that was mass murder. Piracy and murder. Do you think I'm going to let *you* stop me from learning all I can? Do you think I *dare*'—he sneered the word—'make you do a little of the crying those sailors had to do? You've got a chance. They had none.'

He stopped, heavy footsteps sounded outside the door. There was a tap, and Mark Errol's voice called:

'You want us, Bill?'

'Have you got the instruments?'

'Yes,' said Errol.

149

'A moment,' said Loftus.

He kept his eyes on the girl, and almost unwillingly he felt admiration for her. There was a lot to be said for anyone who could be as cool and calm as she.

She said: 'Jim told them not to act until he gave the word. I would have stopped anything like it, or given them away. You can't stop murder with murder. We've been prepared to go a long way—we've had to. But'—she even smiled—'if you think your threats would make me talk, you're quite wrong.'

And Loftus believed her.

For a moment he felt helpless, for he did not know whether he could get information from her by torture. As he stood watching that small, determined face, he told himself that thousands of others, perhaps millions, would die if he relented.

'But I'll tell you what I can,' said Garry Cartwright abruptly. 'After this I suppose I've no choice. Not,' she added helplessly, and now Loftus saw that she was really near despair, 'that you can do anything. If they've got my brother they have the thing itself. And Forster will take him to Germany without losing time, there's not much doubt of that.'

'It won't be easy,' said Loftus.

'Easier than you think.' She shrugged. 'Well—are you going to send the butchers away?'

'When I've heard the story,' said Loftus, and he shrugged. 'But others will want to hear it too. We'll get along to my room.'

As he opened the door, Mark Errol and Davidson stood outside, and they looked a little sheepish. Wally, particularly, for he carried a tray of instruments.

She averted her eyes from the tray.

They walked towards the bigger room. Craigie had just

entered, after a further telephone talk with Wishart. He looked surprised as the girl led the way, and Loftus said:

'We're going to hear a statement, Gordon.'

'Good. The truth I hope,' said Craigie.

'I'll tell you all I can,' said Garry Cartwright. 'Now...'

The Rt. Hon. David Wishart and the Rt. Hon. Winsley Lawrence had not slept that night—and prior to then they had contrived to sleep for an hour or two even in the worst of crises. Scotland Yard was looking for Scott but the task was made doubly difficult by the need for secrecy. The Press could be silenced, up to a point—but even under the censorship there could be leakages of information, the disappearance of Jonathan Scott would create a sensation of the first order.

More...

Scott directed foreign policy.

In the pre-war days the Prime Minister had taken a directing hand, but Scott had been Minister for War in those days. Now Scott was the key man—and his disappearance by itself alone would be disastrous. There were a dozen points of foreign policy demanding urgent attention—which only Scott could give thoroughly and expertly.

It was tragedy.

And, they asked themselves time and time again, there seemed no reason for it. They had no idea who had staged the kidnapping. From Craigie they had heard Loftus's story, or the gist of it. They had heard of the Cartwrights, and of the agent who was reputed to be from Berlin—Forster, who was likely to stop at nothing to get what he wanted.

Had Forster staged the kidnapping?

Or the Cartwrights?

And what did the Cartwrights aim to do?

They had the door ajar, for it was nearly five o'clock, and the room had grown warm. They heard the ring at the front-door bell, and the slow footsteps of the footman going towards it. Wishart started.

'Craigie, I wonder?'

'Probably,' said Lawrence. He changed his cigar from one side of his mouth to the other.

It was Craigie, and with him Loftus. The others knew the big man, and they shook hands. Craigie seemed less tired than he had for some days, and spoke briskly as he sat down.

'We're getting somewhere,' he said. 'I've the Cartwrights' story for you. It has its fantastic points, but it does explain a lot. In the first place, the Nazis did not sink the *Ibrox*.'

'Nonsense,' barked Lawrence.

'It's true. The Cartwrights are members of a small organisation, as wealthy as any small country,' said Craigie, and now that he was repeating the essence of what he had heard from the girl he himself was finding it almost impossible to believe. 'I can't give you names—the girl doesn't know them. She does know that financial magnates from a dozen countries, combatant and neutral, have formed a syndicate to exploit the new lens.'

Wishart said: 'We must find out who they are.'

'It will take time,' said Craigie quietly. 'Well. Cartwright invented the lens. His sister claims that its range is more than ten miles—it hasn't been effectively tested farther than that. Cartwright and his sister are pacifists.'

'What?' shouted Lawrence. 'Pacifists who...'

'And,' went on Craigie, who knew that the best way of handling Lawrence in an obstinate mood was to ignore him, 'they linked up with the syndicate on the understanding that the lens should be developed so as to ensure peace. I told you,' he said, as Lawrence clicked his thumbs sharply against his palms, 'that there was a fantastic angle to it; Lawrence, for heaven's sake let me tell you the story as I know it and don't interrupt.'

Lawrence subsided, and Wishart signed to the Chief to go on.

'The Cartwrights' idea was that a sufficiently strong force could be used to make each combatant country cease hostilities. A power which they could not control, for instance, would make even the big powers stop and think. *But* the weapon had to be absolutely secret and one which none of the warring countries could use.'

'Ye-es,' said Lawrence, and for the first time he seemed impressed. 'Go on.'

'The Cartwrights had the lens, but no money. The brother did the commercial work, getting in touch first with one man and then another. He used agents—friends whom he believed he could trust. He wanted money, of course, but believed he could get it on the basis that the financial interests of most countries and most individuals were being badly affected by the war. Peace would be worth a fortune. Millionaires in industries badly affected by the war would be only too glad to get hold of anything which might bring it to an early end. Cartwright put his proposition to such men and they accepted it. Before any rumour of the thing went out, they had to have everything they wanted to demonstrate effectively. Ships and aeroplanes primarily.'

'Hmm,' said Lawrence, and he jutted his lips forward. 'So the *Ibrox* went down to a pirate?'

Craigie nodded.

'It's the only explanation. Miss Cartwright assures me that only as a last resort was the weapon to be used at sea, and then only after representations were made to the Governments concerned, and turned down—as was expected. But the man Forster, probably a German agent although that is not yet fully established, learned something of it through the secretary of a member of the syndicate. The secretary was murdered. Forster went thoroughly into the lens's potential—as thoroughly as he could in the circumstances, and in the course of his investigations discovered that Professor Grafton claimed to have made a similar discovery.'

'It was on the same lines,' said Wishart.

'It was a flop,' interpolated Lawrence downrightly. 'We tried it out under all conditions, and it was useless.'

'So Cartwright claimed,' said Craigie. 'But Cartwright knew that Grafton was working along the same lines as he had done. Grafton had gone part of the way, but there were some things he had not discovered. Forster knew this too, and Forster presumably kept a watch on Grafton. We know that Grafton's daughter passed some information to a man named Warncliffe. Forster believed that this was dangerous, and attacked Warncliffe. And then we began to take an interest. Now...'

Craigie straightened in his chair. The atmosphere in the room grew tense, for Craigie's manner suggested that he was getting to the crux of the matter.

'Now,' he went on, 'the Cartwrights *knew* everything there was to know about the Department, and that worried us. The girl knew individual members, and the names of others were quite familiar. Few people could have had that information unless from enemy agents of high standing, *or* from equally important officials in this country. Some such official—the girl has not named him—gave the Cartwrights all the necessary information. The syndicate was determined that nothing should allow a leakage of the existence of the lens to reach the ears of the Cabinet.

'All the time, remember, the Cartwrights and the syndicate were aware of the danger from Forster, but they were more anxious to prevent us from learning just what was happening. They wanted to spring this as a complete surprise. But Forster also started to operate against us. The Cartwrights actually *helped* us to avoid trouble from Forster, while trying to prevent us from interfering. Forster came into the open when we showed a greater interest in Grafton, and acted swiftly after this morning's affair. Grafton, one of two living men who can supervise the making of these lenses—which can be adapted to almost any size—was kidnapped this morning, and Cartwright himself was taken tonight. Forster has everything—except the syndicate, and a large supply of the lenses, which are somewhere in England.'

Lawrence broke in excitedly:

'We need those lenses, Craigie, and we need the ship that is fitted with them.'

'We don't know the ship, and we don't know where the lenses are kept,' said Craigie. 'The girl may be lying, but I believe she's right. But we can get what we want.'

'How?' demanded Wishart, sharply.

'Someone gave the Cartwrights information about the Department,' said Craigie. 'And some Englishmen are members of the syndicate. The syndicate, for some reason not yet known, took the initiative while the Cartwrights—the pacifist members—were away. In short, the syndicate has severed itself from the Cartwrights by the sinking of the *Ibrox*. We are likely to be faced with demands in the near future, and'—Craigie shrugged—'for the time being we shall have to accede.'

'I'm damned if we will!' snapped Lawrence. 'I'll have every ship in the Navy hunting for the pirate. We'll find it by day, capture it and keep it afloat. And we will have a ship fitted with the lenses.

'Yes,' said Craigie with a dry smile. 'I believe you will, Lawrence, but it's going to take time. The time element is the one we can't fight against.'

Lawrence scowled.

'And what,' he demanded sarcastically, 'does your Department propose to do about the man Forster?'

'Scotland Yard has issued special instructions for every port to be watched,' said Craigie quietly. 'All coastal patrols, naval or air-force, are keeping watch for anyone trying to get out of the country...'

Lawrence laughed.

'All right. Have *you* any ideas, Loftus?'

'I'm brimful of ideas,' said Bill Loftus. 'Mostly I'm thinking about a man named Warncliffe, who has wandered up and down Europe for some years, and who recently pitched me a very pretty story. Also I'm thinking about Grafton's daughter.'

'That,' said Lawrence sardonically, 'helps a great deal.'

'Probably more than you realise,' said Loftus. 'You see, gentlemen, we've learned and provisionally accept the statement that the Cartwrights acted from the highest of motives, but that the syndicate betrayed their trust. The syndicate would naturally want Grafton watched, as being a man who might steal their thunder. Warncliffe, on his own admission, has taken parts of Grafton's formula from time to time from Janice Grafton...' He seemed to be thinking aloud, and there was some truth in that. 'Warncliffe could be the syndicate's agent and therefore could put us in touch with the syndicate.'

'Where's Warncliffe?' demanded Lawrence.

'Being watched,' said Loftus, and he stood up. 'May I use your telephone, Mr. Wishart? Thanks.'

And he lifted the telephone, and called a Bournemouth number.

17

MORE ACTION IN BOURNEMOUTH

Mark Errol did not know whether to be pleased or sorry. After Loftus and Craigie had heard the girl's story, with Mark and Wally as silent listeners who believed what they heard almost against their will—Loftus had given Mark Errol his stiffest job yet.

He had said casually:

'Mark, look after Miss Cartwright, will you? A prison cell isn't necessary, but get her to the Cliff Royal for a spell. If she shows restlessness, discourage her.'

And that had been that.

Wally had driven them from Winchester while Errol and the girl had sat in the back. They had been silent most of the way; what little conversation had passed between them had been banal, until Mark had said:

'Let's stop pretending, Garry.' He had fallen into the habit of calling her by her Christian name. 'Why did you pick on me at Waterloo?'

'I wanted to give you a warning, and you wouldn't take it.'

'Did you expect me to?'

'I—hoped you would. Or Loftus would. I knew that it wasn't up to you.'

'You knew a lot,' said Mark gruffly.

He was not pleased with life as they ran into Bournemouth, and made for the Cliff Royal. Davidson had only been there by day, and the place was difficult enough to find then. By night and in the black-out it was a positive rabbit warren on the West Cliff, and Mark was compelled to lend a hand with the route-finding. They drew up outside the hotel at last—and from the darkness there loomed a gigantic figure.

'Stand and deliver!' said the figure sepulchrally.

'Go and drown yourself,' snapped Mark, and he proved he was not in the best of tempers.

'Naughty, naughty,' reproved the giant in the same deep voice. 'You're feeling better, I hope, Wally.'

'Tirin' business, that's all,' said Wally Davidson. 'How's life down here, Martin?'

'Slow,' said the giant, one Martin Best. 'On the cold side, too. My orders are to stand around until you arrive, and then take charge of operations.' He went with them—without appearing to notice Garry—to the front door of the hotel. This was unlatched, and when they went inside and the blinds were adjusted, the girl could see Martin Best for what he was.

A vast man, and untidy—the type who contrived to get untidy in a dinner-jacket, and to look badly dressed in a bathing costume. He had a genial, attractive face, with a large and very square chin, a mobile and generous-looking mouth and a tooth-brush moustache—which, of course, needed trimming. His mackintosh hung open, and there was a trail of cigarette ash down his waistcoat.

In the hall was another man—Best's opposite in most things.

Where Best was dark and his hair needed brushing, Bob

Carruthers was as fair as corn, and his hair was immaculate. So was his exquisite grey suit, while his fair-complexioned face was an apt likeness to Adonis. No one suspected that he had been a useful heavy-weight, and at one time had held the amateur title.

He raised a hand negligently.

'Come in, folks, it's time we threw a party.' He smiled winningly at Garry Cartwright, and demanded to be introduced. He was. There was something about the flippancy of the four men which made Garry laugh in spite of herself.

She did not know that the management of the Cliff Royal had been advised that the young men would take up their quarters there until further notice, and that admission must be made possible at all hours of the day and night. And she did not know that Janice Grafton and Edward Grey were still there.

Carruthers was watching Grey, and another agent—a youngster named Lister, renowned for his freckles—was watching Janice. From the outside of her door, he had been apt to stay gloomily. Mark Errol had been watching the Professor, but was now a free agent, as was Davidson. Some half a mile away a tubby man with red hair—one Jock Allison—was keeping watch on Warncliffe's flat, while yet another of Craigie's young men was at hand to follow Warncliffe's servant, Paul, if Paul left the flat.

Nothing, Carruthers reported, had happened. They gathered together in the lounge, with Lister keeping a watch upstairs; and there was beer.

'You'll join us?' Carruthers asked Garry. 'Or if you'd rather have a sherry we can manage it. Otherwise it's got to be grape-fruit.'

'Grape-fruit,' said Garry Cartwright firmly.

'I was afraid so,' said Carruthers. 'That nasty look in your eyes warned me.' He poured grape-fruit, and then beer. 'Well, gentlemen, do we sleep or what?'

'It looks like "or what",' said Best.

'Miss Cartwright needs some sleep,' said Errol quietly. 'My room's empty, isn't it?'

'No one's there as far as I know,' said Carruthers.

'Right—you'd better get up soon,' Mark said, and his air was almost fatherly. Garry shrugged, and Carruthers and Best demanded—as was inevitable—to know what was happening. Wally told the story as well as he could and Garry Cartwright was surprised by the calm acceptance of the narrative which Best and Carruthers showed. They appeared neither startled nor scared, and took it as a matter of course.

Mark stood up abruptly.

'Coming, Garry?'

She nodded, and there was a chorus of good nights. Mark stepped into the hall after her, and was startled to see tears filming her eyes. He felt for a moment completely nonplussed, and they reached the stairs without a word.

She walked easily, and with grace. She was so clean-cut, normally so self-possessed, so unfeminine in her reaction to the rushed events of the past few hours, that tears were the last thing he had expected. Halfway up the stairs he said stiffly:

'What is it?' A pause. 'Your brother?'

Her response startled him.

'Are they always like that?'

'They? Oh, the crowd? Yes, pretty well always the same. I haven't been with them long, but I've never known them any different. They're like it in the middle of a shindy, or when they're doing nothing.'

'Nothing frightens them?'

'I wouldn't say that. But they hide it. Nothing seems,' he said, 'to frighten you.'

'*Seems!*' There was a wealth of scorn in her voice. 'Oh, I've been scared to death a dozen times since Jim found this beastly thing! I thought once that we were really going to get away with it. Peace for all time,' she said very softly yet bitterly. 'I was a fool, all kinds of a damned fool! There'll be no such thing! All the work Jim and I have done is absolutely wasted. If we'd brought this thing to the Government immediately we would have brought peace a lot nearer. This accursed syndicate looks as if it's going to squeeze every penny it can out of England. I've been afraid that the money angle would bring the crash, but Jim seemed so certain that the syndicate was genuine.'

'Well,' said Mark awkwardly, 'things do turn out that way. Don't you know a single member of the syndicate?'

'Not one.'

'But you've been in your brother's confidence in practically everything else.'

'I didn't approve of the method of finance, and he sensed that. When he makes his mind up it's not easily altered. He felt that I wasn't to be relied on with the syndicate, and decided to negotiate with it himself.

'How has it been negotiated?'

'By telephone, or when Jim's called on one or the other of them. He's had a messenger several times.'

'Do you know him?'

'Not by name.'

'Would you recognise him again?'

'Oh, yes.'

'That might help,' said Mark. He pushed open the door of his room, and unthinkingly stepped through, sitting on the end of one of the twin beds—that which Mike had been using before the morning outrage. For the first time Garry hesitated, and her lips curved a little. 'It might help,' Mark repeated, and lit a cigarette. 'Garry—quite seriously. Are you telling us all you know?'

'Yes. All that will help.'

'Why?'

She shrugged. 'Well, the sinking of the ship was enough to make the difference—I'd dreaded something like that. And then—well, Loftus and Craigie seemed so certain about themselves. You and Davidson do, for that matter. You don't seem to have any doubt about you're being right. I've hated this Government since I can remember—and so has Jim. We're not exactly Communists, I don't think you could even call us Socialists. But there's something grievously wrong with the present systems, or war would be impossible. Our one thought has been to make it so. Now...' She looked pale and harassed. 'So far as I can see, Loftus and the others will do more than Jim and I will ever do.'

Mark smiled.

'Garry: Loftus and Craigie and the rest of them have been trying to stop war for years. But in our odd way, and despite the wires that get pulled, and the different interests that have to be studied, it looks as if Britain has managed to strike the best way of getting some kind of decent social order. Not a Union of the British Empire, or drivel like that—but we *are* better than most countries, and if we've been a gang of pirates in the past, at least the countries we stole have self-government, and better treatment than any others. However, we're getting on the heavy side, and it's late.'

'Ye-es,' said Garry. 'Odd, isn't it? You can see a thing so clearly all your life, and then suddenly see it differently. When—it's too late.'

Mark said: 'It's a long way from too late yet—Loftus will get results before long.'

'I wonder. He seemed too slow at the Manor.'

'He'd some idea that he didn't talk about, and as far as I've gathered the police made a major error when they ignored him. Loftus gets through, Garry. I doubt if he's worried about the situation half as much as you are, and I'll offer what odds you like that he'll be busy before the night's over. We'll get some sleep. I can't offer you pyjamas, but there's a spare pair of my cousin's. 'Night.'

'Good night, Mark.' She smiled a little, and as he reached the door, she said: 'I've been watching you for some days, at different clubs and places. Before you went abroad. We were afraid all the time that the Department would step in.'

'Nothing personal meant,' Mark said with a grin.

'No-o.'

'At the moment,' said Mark, 'we're both too tired to worry about it.'

He re-entered the room downstairs with a more jaunty air than he had left it, and he made remarks about the fug of smoke and beer fumes.

'Hear ye,' grinned Martin Best. 'He comes from the purity of her proximity.'

The telephone—fitted to the lounge that afternoon—burred sharply. Wally lifted it, and from the other end heard Loftus beginning to spell his name backwards.

'Right, Bill.'

'How many of you there?' asked Loftus.

'Four in this room—Lister's upstairs, and...'

'Four will be enough. Keep an eye on Grey, but the rest of you worry about Warncliffe. Now listen...'

Mr. Jeremiah Warncliffe should have been sleeping.

Instead, he was sitting in his dressing-room in front of a

radio-receiving set which had no loud-speaker. Earphones were clamped over his head, and he was leaning back and smoking. There was no sound in the room but his even breathing—and that of his man Paul. Paul was sitting, just as much at his ease but in a lounge suit, and smoking a cigar.

'Aren't they through yet?' He spoke testily as Warncliffe yawned.

'No—they won't be long. You needn't wait up.'

'Thanks. I propose to.'

'Please yourself,' said Warncliffe. He continued to listen speaking at the same time. 'You were a damned fool not to show up after the explosion this morning. Loftus spotted it in a flash.'

Paul's oddly good-looking face—mask-like, for it lacked every expression—did not change. But there was a note of venom in his voice.

'You made enough mistakes, God knows! Loftus guessed what you'd been doing.'

'So you listened, did you?'

'It's my job to,' snapped Paul. 'If they knew what you'd done this morning, you'd last about twenty-four hours.'

Warncliffe sneered: 'Who's going to tell them?'

'I'm not—while you keep up the payments,' said Paul.

Warncliffe's body tightened, and he leaned forward towards the radio, as if getting closer would help him to hear better. He heard the message that was sent over the radio on a short-wave station which few people ever caught. It was in code and he wrote swiftly. Paul leaned forward, reading the message and translating from memory. Paul's eyes, very cold and grey, glittered as the message came to an end.

'They've got it! Got the *Ibrox*!'

'My God!' breathed Warncliffe. He waited, but the message

was signed off, and he took the earphones from his head and stood up abruptly. 'When was it?'

'At eight o'clock tonight! I...'

And then he stopped.

Paul swung round in his chair, and his hand went towards his coat pocket—but he did not draw out his gun. For two men were standing in the doorway, and one of them carried a Thompson sub-machine-gun.

The second was tall, and pale-faced—and dressed in black.

Warncliffe licked his lips.

'What—what the hell's this?'

'Don't you recognise me, Warncliffe? There was a sibilant note to the man's voice—he had a natural difficulty with the 's' and because of it his voice would always be recognisable. 'I'm Forster. I've come for you.'

In the bright light his face seemed even paler than it was, and against it his lips showed vividly red—unnaturally red lips for a man. His eyes, too, were bright and very vivid: they were light blue, not unlike Paul's. His face was very lean and the features seemed carved from stone because of the regularity of the features.

Warncliffe was sweating.

His brown-plaid dressing-gown sagged, and his hands were in sight, clenching convulsively. He could not keep his eyes off the men in the doorway.

'But...'

'You made too many mistakes,' said Forster. 'You tried to work with me, and you were also working for the others. This syndicate!' he snapped, and the sibilance grew more pronounced. 'Understand, Warncliffe, I work for my country, not for money. You...'

'I—I'll do what I can,' muttered Warncliffe, and his lips

were unsteady. 'I've done plenty for you. I didn't know it was you in person but I've done it through others.'

'For money,' Forster said. 'It has been useful, the Führer has found it worth paying for—but there is only one thing left to do with a man who works for two sides.'

He stopped, and raised a hand.

The man at his side raised the Tommy-gun—and Warncliffe jumped from his chair, screaming. Paul sat cowering back in his; a second passed that seemed unending.

And then the machine-gun opened fire.

Two bullets struck Warncliffe—but only two. The third went into the floor, like a dozen others. Then the man holding it dropped it and crumpled up—while Forster swung round towards the stairs, and Paul made a leap for the window in a desperate effort to get away.

Warncliffe lay on the floor, with blood coming from wounds in his chest.

18

VERSUS THE SYNDICATE

At the head of the stairs, and facing Forster, was Wally
Davidson with a smoking automatic in his right hand.
Behind Wally was Mark Errol. Unseen, but in support, were
Carruthers and Best.

There was a split-second of silence, broken only by the
final clatter of the Tommy-gun. Then Forster put his hand to
his face—and he moved swiftly towards the lights which were
controlled by a switch close to his hand.

'I think not,' said Wally coolly.

He fired again—and a bullet cracked into the back of
Forster's hand. But it did not stop the German, whose almost
nerveless fingers touched the switch. It went upwards—and
darkness fell abruptly—darkness which meant nothing to
Forster, for he was wearing the glasses which he had put on in
that split-second.

His left hand pulled a gun from his pocket, and he kicked
the door to. He fired twice towards the head of the stairs,
and the darkness was split for a moment by the bluish-
yellow light that spat out. He heard a shout as he went

through into Warncliffe's room, banging the door behind him.

He kept his injured hand pressed against his chest, to stop the blood as much as he could. In the clear-blue light ahead of him because of the glasses he saw Warncliffe, who was not moving but whose eyes were wide open, and who seemed agonised.

He stepped over Warncliffe's body, reached the window and saw the ladder which was being pushed slowly against the sill. A split-second later the beam of a torch shone upwards, and he knew that the attack was coming from both quarters.

And then the door was flung open.

Another beam shot across the room, from the torch in Wally Davidson's hand. Wally saw the man standing there, and fired—and then darted to one side. Forster pressed the trigger of his gun, and the bullet struck the torch from Davidson's hand. Wally swore as the blackness descended again, and pitched forward. The second bullet from Forster's gun hit the floor between his legs.

'Steady!' he roared, for Errol's benefit.

Forster pushed out his free hand, lodging the gun in his coat, and heaved against the ladder. A torch-beam caught him, but he dodged back in time to avoid a bullet, and contrived to send the ladder backwards. Carruthers, who had been on the fourth rung, leapt for safety. The ladder crashed down, and there was an oath from Allison—the fourth member of the party.

On the floor, Davidson hesitated—then caught the reflection of a light against the window, and saw Forster for a split-second.

He fired twice.

Forster's answering fire came, and Wally winced as a bullet cut across his shoulders like a red-hot needle. But he kept his finger on the trigger, sending four bullets towards the German, who was against the wall and close to the window. The second and third bullets hit their targets, getting Forster below the knee each time. Forster crashed. From behind Wally came Mark Errol, switching on the light and firing as Forster made a final effort with his gun. Mark's bullet struck the barrel of it, and Forster's hand was wrenched away.

It was hard to believe that it had happened and that it was over. Mark Errol stood staring at Forster, who was wounded in three places. He looked like a man who had gone mad.

And Mark saw Warncliffe, stretched out, with blood at the corners of his mouth.

'Not—so—good,' said Wally Davidson.

'What's the trouble?' demanded Martin Best.

He came in through the window, for the ladder had been picked up. Below, Carruthers was nursing a wrenched knee after the fall from the ladder, and Allison was making sure that Paul did not get away. On the floor of Warncliffe's shattered lounge Davidson sat with a rueful expression on his face, mingled with pain.

'Hold Forster,' Mark snapped, and in that moment he assumed command of the situation, much as Loftus would have done. 'Don't try moving about, Wally, until we've had a look at your back.' He knelt down, then, by Warncliffe's side, and he eased the man's head to a cushion which he took from one of the chairs. Warncliffe was breathing stertorously, and it was obvious that he had not much longer to live.

'A—drink,' he gasped. 'Water...'

Errol glanced round, and saw a water-jug standing close to a decanter of whisky. He fetched it, and poured a little water into the man's mouth. Warncliffe licked his lips, and his saliva was tinged with blood.

'Tell Loftus—he was—right. I've been taking—Grafton's—

papers for—the syndicate. Passing 'em—over. Know—the syndicate?'

'Name one or two,' said Errol.

'Can't,' said Warncliffe simply. 'Damned careful—and clever. Send messages to—Regal Hotel. That's all.'

'But the name...'

'Smith—just Smith.' Warncliffe's lips twisted with a sudden spasm of pain, and when it was over he breathed more heavily and his eyes were closed. 'Very clever, the—syndicate. I've worked for them—long time. Worked for Berlin, too. Up and down—Europe. Forster's a big shot in their—es-es-espionage. I made the mistake of—playing on both—sides.'

'Yes,' said Errol. 'But what about this man Smith?'

'Never seen him. Only send letters. A. Smith. Cart—Cartwright's all right. Damned—fool, that's all. Only motive worth working for here is—money. All I've—ever done. I...' He stopped short with another spasm of pain, and Errol doubted whether he would ever speak again. But he did.

'You will—tell Jan—I—was all for—her?'

'I'll tell her,' promised Errol.

'Th-thanks. Advise her not—marry—Grey. Pompous—ass, Grey. Jan—Jan—*Janice!*'

That was the last word that he spoke.

Despite the explosion of the morning, those few people who had remained in Redfern Mansions were not easily disturbed. Those who were did not leave their room to investigate the disturbance, and thus it was that only an A.R.P. warden on his nightly prowl showed any interest in what was happening—and when the curtain was drawn across the window from which light was streaming, he walked on.

Allison, his red hair dishevelled and his plump frame enveloped in a Teddy-bear coat, had brought Paul in. The servant looked scared—but it did not seem as if he would be persuaded to talk easily. Forster's wounds had been cleansed and patched up, and Davidson was lying stomach downwards on a settee, while Mark Errol cleaned the wound that ran across his shoulder. Carruthers came in, limping. 'Bill was there, and he's flying down at once,' he said. 'Can you spare a moment?'

He hobbled to the door, and Best followed him out, with Mark Errol, Davidson groaned, and Allison shrugged. Obviously there was news, and Carruthers did not want Forster or Paul to know what it was.

He pulled the door which led to the dining-room close. 'You're to try to get what story you can out of Forster. We're to have another cut at Garry Cartwright,' Carruthers added quietly, 'and we're to see what Grafton's daughter and the man say when they're really under pressure.'

Allison took Paul along by foot, while Martin Best lifted Forster bodily into a car, and drove towards the Cliff Royal. Errol and Carruthers stayed behind at the flat for twenty minutes, searching every corner; they discovered nothing that would be of interest to Loftus.

That job finished, Mark contacted with the police.

Special Home Office orders had been received in the area, and there was no difficulty. A police-surgeon and an inspector, with the usual complement of fingerprint and camera men, arrived. Errol and Carruthers went in the latter's car to the Cliff Royal, while the surgeon dressed Davidson's back.

'You'll be all right,' he said, 'but you won't be able to move in a hurry for a few days.'

'I never do move in a hurry,' said Wally sadly.

The others had been busy. Carruthers had spent twenty

minutes with Garry Cartwright, and could not shake her story. Martin Best handled Janice Grafton. Disturbed in the early hours, startled but not frightened, she had sat in an arm-chair in her room, with a dressing-gown about her slim figure.

'I told Mr. Loftus all I knew,' she said. 'Don't you think you owe me some kind of explanation for this?'

'A thousand explanations,' said Best. 'Loftus is the man for that. I hope we won't have to disturb you again tonight.'

'If you have to it can't be helped,' she said. 'Mr. Best—is there no news of my father?'

'None at all,' said Martin honestly.

When he closed the door, he said *sotto voce* that he was glad he had not the task of breaking the news of Warncliffe's death.

Mark had questioned Forster, with more results than he had anticipated. Paul proved sullen, and would not speak. Mark then went into Janice Grafton's room. She was still sitting in the easy-chair. Her hair was in a net which somehow did not make it look too set: and she looked a delight.

Mark offered her a cigarette. She took one, and leaned forward to get a light. Her eyes were very clear, and her hand was steady. Mark cleared his throat as he flicked the match away.

'You've some news,' she said.

'Yes.'

'My father?' Her voice remained steady.

'No. Miss Grafton, you and Mr. Warncliffe between you told a story to Mr. Loftus this morning—and the story in many respects was not true.'

She stared, her eyes widening.

'As far as I knew, it was true.'

'You had no idea that Warncliffe was working for a syndicate planning to rob your father of whatever good there might be in his discovery.'

'I don't believe it!' she said flatly, and stood up. 'I would trust Jerry anywhere—anywhere! He told the whole truth, I know that.'

'I'm sorry,' Mark said. 'He has confirmed that it was a lie, Miss Grafton, in front of several witnesses, and at a time when most men can be expected to tell the truth. He gave me a message for you. He asked me to say that he was "all for Jan"; they were his exact words. Do you understand?'

She stood quite still, the colour draining from her face.

'When was this?'

'A little more than an hour ago.'

'I—see,' she said, and he could hardly hear her words. 'So you killed him. You—killed—Jerry.'

Mark said more roughly:

'He was shot by Forster, a Nazi agent, and Warncliffe was dealing with him, and with other people who are after your father's invention as well.'

'What do you mean?' Janice demanded.

'We believed Forster had kidnapped your father. He denies this. I have every reason to believe him, and that suggests that Warncliffe may have been a party to it. And you,' added Mark very soberly. 'Do you understand? *You* and Warncliffe.'

19

WHERE IS THE PROFESSOR?

L oftus arrived at the Bournemouth airfield, at Hurn, just after six o'clock. Dawn was breaking when a driver met him off the plane, and he was driven to the Cliff Royal. As he entered, Martin Best greeted him cheerily, and Loftus lifted a hand in greeting.

'Where's Mark?'

'His own room I think—Number 11. It's been rather bad. Jan Grafton nearly collapsed soon after learning that Warncliffe had died, and she tried to kill herself.'

Loftus pursed his lips.

'Did she, then.'

He went up the stairs two at a time, and tapped on the door of Number 11 before going in. Janice was lying in bed, her head propped on pillows, two spots of red on either cheek. Garry Cartwright was sitting at her side, and putting a cold flannel on her forehead.

She looked dully at Loftus. 'Go away, please.'

'I won't stay long,' Loftus promised, but he sat on the edge of the bed. 'Miss Grafton, I must ask you two questions. Are you sure that your father had failed to perfect his lens?'

'As far as I know, yes.' Her voice was utterly weary and dispirited.

'You can't be positive?'

'No—not absolutely. But I think he was more worried than ever by the papers that were stolen last night.'

'You know some were stolen?'

'Oh, yes. I pretended there hadn't been because—because I didn't want...'

She stopped, and her expression was piteous as she looked into Loftus's face. Garry exclaimed:

'Must you?'

'Miss Grafton,' said Loftus in the same dead-level voice. 'You didn't want Warncliffe to be suspected.'

'That's—right.' They could hardly hear her answer.

'What made you think he would be?'

'Jerry was always short of money, that was why I helped him to get what he could! The lens was father's idea, but he would never have made money out of it. Teddy would make sure of that. Teddy's shrewd where money's concerned, he...' She paused and went on more quietly: 'What does it matter? I've come to hate Teddy, he's always so right, he's so clever with money, and he had Father just where he wanted him. It was Teddy who put Father against Jerry in the first place. He was always saying that Jerry was—was an adventurer. If Jerry was helping Forster, he believed it was right!'

'Yes,' lied Loftus soberly. 'I'm sure he did, Miss Grafton. I'm sorry it's been necessary to worry you, but there's only one more question. Warncliffe was in touch with other people besides Forster. Do you know them?'

'No—I'd no idea.'

'Right,' said Loftus. 'I needn't worry you any more. Mark, will you spare me a minute?'

Martin Best and Carruthers were in the lounge, which looked like the morning after a stag-party. Loftus took a chair near a fire which had been neglected, poked it a little, and looked across at Mark.

'Well?'

Mark gave him a résumé of what had happened, and the results of the various interrogations. Only Grey now seemed a doubtful quantity, and Mark said:

'I've had a word with him. He hated Warncliffe, and actually admitted being glad he's dead. He said he had no idea of the kidnapping of Grafton until after it had happened, but I'm not sure that he was telling the truth.'

'He was marking time,' said Carruthers.

'Let's go and see if I can make him run,' said Loftus. He reached the door of Grey's room, and turned the handle. He pushed—and the door did not open. He pushed again, and he stared at Mark.

'Was it locked last time?'

'No.'

'Huh!' said Loftus, and put his shoulder to the door. At the second attempt the bolt on the other side of the door gave way, and he staggered into the room. Mark followed swiftly, gun in hand.

But he did not need it.

The grey light of early morning filtered through the drawn curtains, showing that the room was in utter disorder. Clothes were strewn everywhere, a table was overturned, and the wardrobe was pulled away from the wall.

But what mattered most was the man on the bed.

Mark recognised Grey—and a Grey whose face was

turning colour, for about his neck was tied a scarf, drawn cruelly tight. His chest was heaving in the effort to breathe.

Within half an hour Grey was sitting up in bed. He could remember nothing, he said, except that he had felt someone fingering his throat, had awakened and been chloroformed. There was the faintest of odours of chloroform about his mouth and nose, and a tiny purplish stain on a pillow.

'After that—you came in,' said Grey. 'I don't know how to thank you, Mr. Loftus. I'm deeply grateful, believe me.'

'That's all right,' said Loftus breezily. 'Why was the attack made, Mr. Grey?'

'It's all a part of this outrageous interference with Professor Grafton. Warncliffe arranged it, I've no doubt of that—or someone for whom he worked.'

'Do you know he had associates?'

'Of course he had!' snapped Grey. 'The man was in the pay of some country or other, I never doubted that.'

They could get nothing more out of him, and Errol and he went out. On the landing Errol raised his brows.

'Phoney or not?' he asked.

'Very suspiciously like it,' said Loftus. 'He choked and chloroformed himself, of course, staged it for our benefit.'

'If you're so sure, why the devil did you let him think he'd fooled you?'

'I want him to believe that he put it across. I want him to think that we're very sorry for him, and that we know he was attacked by many wicked men. I want him to believe that we take him at his own estimate—the soul of righteousness. I also want,' added Loftus casually, 'to know just why he did it, and what he knows about Grafton and the new lens.'

Mark shrugged.

'You could have forced it out of him.'

'Possibly,' shrugged Loftus. 'We'll see. Well now, friends and brothers.' He glanced round the lounge, where Carruthers, Best, Davidson—sitting on a chair bolt upright so that he did not touch it with his back—were also sitting, while Lister and Allison watched outside the hotel. 'You will get all the rest you can, except the man who's watching Grey.'

'What about the girls?' asked Mark.

'We'll have a nurse in for Janice Grafton. Garry's coming back to Town with me. I want to see the mysterious Mr. A. Smith, who goes from time to time to the Regal Hotel, Piccadilly. We also want your report on the talk with Forster.'

'It's ready.' Mark passed over a paper which he took from his breast pocket. 'Coded, of course. It looks to me as if Forster could tell you a lot about Warncliffe and the syndicate if you worked on him properly.'

'He's given you something,' said Loftus. 'If he *knows* who's got the lens he won't tell us, because we would use it against his country—and Forster won't talk when that's at stake. Now listen. Things should be fairly quiet down here now. Have Grey watched closely, and I'll see that the nurse who comes doesn't let Janice out of her sight.'

'Damn it, she's all right!'

'She might,' said Loftus tentatively, 'be in danger of some kind, Marko.'

Garry, warned that she was to travel, was dressed soon after half-past seven.

'We'll breakfast in London,' Loftus said. 'We'll be there in an hour by air.'

During the flight he studied Forster's statement, and put it in his pocket without comment. Sitting back in the corner of

the car which met them at the airport he looked sideways at
the girl.

'Forster seems to have known about your arrangements
with the syndicate. In fact his story coincides with yours. The
one thing he failed to get, as far as I can tell, is the names of
the members of the syndicate.

'Forster states that after leaving the Manor his car was
attacked, and your brother was taken by others. Presumably
the syndicate. Forster also says that he had regained
consciousness by then.'

The girl's eyes shone.

'Thank God,' said Garry Cartwright.

There was a moment of silence, before Loftus went on.

'Well, now. If Cartwright is with the syndicate, and does
not approve of the sinking of the destroyer, he won't be popular. Grafton is probably with them also. Some of them, we've
good reason to believe, are at sea. There's a thing you've never
told me, you know—and I didn't ask before.'

'What is it?'

'The name of the armed vessel.'

The girl stared at him for some seconds, and then she lifted
her hands helplessly from her lap.

'Oh, it's so absurd. I don't know...'

'A moment,' said Loftus. 'No country in this world is likely
to allow the arming of a vessel in time of war without
reporting it. As far as we're concerned this ship could belong
to the enemy, but Forster's activities put that out. It could not
have been fitted-up in a combatant port, and it's not likely to
have been fitted in a neutral one.'

'I suppose so. What are you driving at?'

'To me,' said Loftus, 'it looks as if this ship might be a
regular warship, belonging to some nation or other—a neutral
nation—and fitted while at sea with the glass lenses. It also

seems to me that your brother, and for that matter yourself, would hardly be satisfied with help from a money-syndicate without any practical means of assisting you in the drive for peace. But a small neutral country might be considered. He's been negotiating with Vania, hasn't he?'

'Good—*God!*' gasped the girl.

'Thanks,' said Loftus dryly. 'A small neutral country which because of its size has always been in danger of aggression. What a beautiful position for it to be able to shake its fists at the belligerents? To sink a British ship, a Russian, and a German—and then to give a warning-off note. *That* was your brother's idea, wasn't it?'

She said haltingly: 'Yes. But how did you know?'

'I didn't believe from the first that you and Cartwright would rely solely on financial help, and when the sinking was reported Vania seemed the one and only nation. Moreover— the Foreign Secretary was the one man in this country who might have learned that Vania was getting too big for its boots. Hence his disappearance.'

'Has Scott been *kidnapped?*'

'He has,' said Loftus. 'It wouldn't surprise me to hear that other Foreign Secretaries are kidnapped before the day's out. I wouldn't be surprised if your guess isn't the true one, Garry. For you, bad luck.'

'What—do you mean?' she said in a strangled voice.

'That Vania accepted the invitation, that the syndicate reached an understanding with the Vanian Government,' said Loftus very slowly. 'That instead of using their weapon to promote peace they're going to try enforcing it as victors. One little country against a dozen big Powers. That's why you were at such pains to keep it secret, why your brother had such confidence. Misplaced confidence, I'm afraid, Garry. Vania will seek victory by force before many days are past.'

She believed it, with him...

Loftus was not even perturbed when, half an hour later, Craigie told him that the French Foreign Minister and the German counterpart were missing from Paris and Berlin respectively.

Which could only precede an ultimatum.

2 0
'DAVID AMONG NATIONS'

The three most sensational kidnappings of recent times had been carried out almost simultaneously. Scott from England, Ariel from Paris, and von Holstein from Berlin. And that was not all, for Dagliov, the Soviet Foreign Minister, who had been on a visit to Leningrad in an effort to stir the Russian troops out of the lethargy that had fallen on them after the effective opposition of the Finns, was also kidnapped.

The four men were smuggled out of their respective countries by air on the evening of their kidnapping—smuggling which had been comparatively easy in view of the fact that the kidnappers could see in the dark. Each man was flown to Vania, each was treated with exemplary courtesy.

It was Sibilla, the Vanian Prime Minister, who interviewed them together in the Palace of Kings at Venn, the Vanian capital. He talked in French, the language which all four men knew well, with a quiet assumption of confidence which had a considerable effect. He delivered an ultimatum. Virtually, Vania held the four major warring Powers at the point of a gun. He acted as the representative of a David among nations, and after he had talked for two hours he had each Foreign Minister conducted to a bedroom and told them that they would be free to return to their own countries on the following day.

Scott was the only man to comment.

'We know what you can do, and this isn't a time for counter-threats. But why waste time? I can be back in London in four hours.'

Sibilla was a tall, thin, grey-bearded man who looked like a French aristocrat and who dressed in the French fashion of the late 'nineties—in tails, a semi-Gladstonian collar and a black cravat held in place by a solitaire diamond ring. His red lips parted in a smile that gave Jonathan Scott little consolation.

'You do not appear to understand. *We* are making the arrangements. It may appear a waste of time to you, but we consider it necessary.'

'Are *we* allowed to consult each other tonight?' asked Scott.

And it was in the small hours of that night that news reached Berlin of one of the major and certainly the most mysterious reverses of the war. The pocket-battleship *Admiral von Bohn* was sunk in mid-Atlantic *under cover of darkness*. In Berlin there was alarm and despondency.

Moscow, about the same time, suffered the heaviest reverse of their war with Finland. The Kronstadt naval and air base was bombed in a dark night, and the bombs were dropped with such accuracy that fifty planes, two destroyers, and two petrol dumps were completely destroyed. Not long afterwards the French aircraft-carrier *Dupress* was sunk by submarine action on a night which was dull and overcast, and when visibility had been negligible. The wires hummed between London and Paris, and Malladet, the French Prime Minister, flew to London.

* * *

'It would appear, then,' said Malladet in his clear but curiously precise English, 'that in your opinion, my friend, the Vanian Government considers itself able to dictate any terms it desires. Is that so?'

'It is possible,' said Wishart cautiously. The contrast between the tall, stately looking Englishman and the solid, chunky Frenchman who could not hide—and did not wish to hide—the traces of his peasant ancestry, was remarkable. Wishart looked more French than Malladet, and Malladet would have passed anywhere as an Englishman.

'It can be taken as certain,' said Craigie.

'But so much of it is guess-work.' Malladet looked at Loftus, who smiled amiably and began to stuff his pipe.

'Hardly guess-work, M'sieu Malladet. There is every reason to assume that it is a fact. I have been carefully into every angle of the situation, and innumerable factors make it less an assumption than a reasoned deduction. The success of the modern David is remarkable only because it has been kept so closely secret. Within twelve hours you will have word from M'sieu Ariel, we shall have news from Mr. Scott. We shall learn that Vania has equipped all her fighting services with the new lenses, and we'll know that by night we're virtually at her mercy.'

Malladet stared. Wishart drew a sharp inward breath, and Craigie fiddled with the stem of his meerschaum.

'Are you *insane?*' demanded Malladet. 'At the mercy of Vania, of *Sibilla?* No, it is nonsense!'

'I'm afraid that it's reasonable,' said Craigie.

'The Service experts will agree,' said Loftus quietly, 'that unless we can counter the effects of the lens by night we shall be well advised to make terms, whatever they are.'

Loftus stopped abruptly, for across his mind there flashed a solution to much of the mystery, a solution to the trouble with Grafton, to Forster's determination to get at Warncliffe before the man could obtain all Grafton's formulae. The idea grew apace as he stared at Malladet.

'My dear M'sieu Loftus...'

'A minute, please,' said Loftus. 'Of course, the effect of the weapon will be cancelled out if more than one country has it. Vania—and the syndicate of which you have heard—holds Cartwright, the inventor, and Grafton, the other man who was reputed to know what comprised the glass. Germany may have some samples of it, but I understand that that will not help them much. We've some samples, and they're being thoroughly examined by our own experts. The key people, however, are Cartwright and Grafton.' He looked at Wishart and then at Malladet, and he spoke with a conviction which was impressive. 'Gentlemen, I would like a word with Mr. Craigie, and then your permission to leave for a while.'

Wishart hesitated. Malladet said sharply:

'Of course, M'sieu.'

'Thank you. Gordon...'

In the passage outside Loftus conducted a brief conversation with his chief, and then was driven rapidly to 55g, Clarges Street. In his flat found Garry Cartwright reading and smoking.

'Well?' she started up.

'Scott's not back, Ariel's disappeared, and it's a safe bet that Dagliov and von Holstein are missing. Are you convinced yet that you've gone the wrong way about it? That this war's got to be finished, and the Allies have to win it, before there can be any hope of permanent peace? Or do you still think Vania will act as a fairy godmother?'

Garry said: 'You were right, of course.'

'Prepared to help to break the Vanian hold?'

'Yes.'

'Right,' said Loftus. 'We're going to Vania.'

'But...'

'Right now, and by air,' said Loftus. 'You're going to telephone Sibilla, the Prime Minister there, and tell him you're free, but you must talk to your brother. He'll invite you over.'

'And then?'

'We'll see,' said Loftus.

Before Loftus and Garry reached Venn, Jonathan Scott and Ariel were in London—the latter's plane diverging after a broadcast request from Malladet. In Number 10 it was Scott who confirmed all that Loftus had suggested—Scott who in his downright way said sharply:

'Sibilla didn't beat about the bush. Practically every Vanian merchant ship of over five thousand tons is armed and fitted with the glass. They're in every part of the Seven Seas. The Navy, for what it's worth, is spread round—officially it's been convoying their merchantmen, actually it's been getting ready for this. The Air Force can strike at any one of the four capitals without much trouble. If we start a major action by day, we can't get through the night. We've got to talk turkey, Wishart.'

'What are the terms?' asked Wishart.

'The immediate cessation of all hostilities. The immediate withdrawal of *all* countries' nationals to those countries. The immediate despatch of all ships of war of all warring countries to Vanian ports and Vanian water *under Vanian control*. The immediate...' Jonathan Scott was talking mechanically, while the four men listening—Wishart, Malladet, Ariel and Craigie—

were staring at him with their expressions strained. 'The immediate surrender of all fighting aircraft to Vanian territory, and the shipment as soon as possible of all heavy arms, guns, and tanks to Vania. In short,' added Scott, and he talked like a man in a dream, 'we give everything to Vania, and Sibilla talks of policing the world. Oh, he made it sound beautiful! We've had our chances and lost them, now the smaller countries are going to have their turn. But behind Sibilla and Vania are these financial interests—this syndicate Loftus talked about. Sibilla wants us disarmed, and then he'll give us our orders. He hinted that France has no business in Africa, we've no business in India. The self-governing dominions he will be pleased to leave as they are,' shouted Scott, and he lifted a clenched hand high above his head. 'We're finished if we give way! All of us! Vania will dictate a damned sight more effectively than Russia or Germany. We've *got* to fight.'

'While we're fighting each other,' Wishart said slowly.

'When we *can't* fight in the dark,' said Malladet abruptly.

'The result will be the same, except that we shall lose millions of men and women,' said Ariel. 'We must come to terms. If the terms are dictated we can do nothing about it.'

'What was the time limit, Jonathan?' Craigie asked.

His quiet voice, almost homely as he addressed the Foreign Minister, did something to ease the tension.

'Twenty-four hours.'

'Then I suggest that Messieurs Malladet and Ariel consult their Governments, and that we call a special meeting of the War Cabinet,' said Craigie. 'In an emergency Parliament can be summoned within twelve hours. And meanwhile Loftus has gone to Vania to negotiate. He is a remarkable man, and may succeed.' When he reached his Whitehall office he sat back in an easy-chair in front of the fire which rarely went out, and closed his eyes wearily.

The work of a generation had been destroyed when the war had started—and now it seemed that the Department and all that the Department stood for was to be destroyed. A David had risen among nations, a David which would dictate its own terms, which would be the terms of a victorious aggressor. He was in no doubt of that. Among the financial backers of the little country were men from England, Germany, Russia and America—from every country in the world. Beneath the cloak of good intentions Vania was to take all and give nothing.

World dictatorship.

It was possible, Craigie knew...

And only Loftus, flying towards Vania alone, but for the sister of the man who had made this possible, could stop the catastrophe.

21

THE SYNDICATE OF POWER

Sibilla entered the Senate House of Vania at nine o'clock on the morning following the despatch of the ultimatum to the major Powers. Only Europe was so far affected; there had been no suggestion of holding a gun at the heads of the Americans—but in the mind of Sibilla there was the conviction that such a day would come. Here was a man with unbridled ambition—a man combining the ruthlessness of Stalin and Hitler, a man with a dream of a world state more fantastic then theirs only because of the smallness of the country he controlled.

First, money had been needed.

In a small chamber of the Senate when he entered the building were forty men, representing the largest financial combines in the world. There were representatives from Britain, France, America, Russia—where the shibboleth of Communism had been evaded for a long time—there were representatives from Japan and China, Turkey and India, from the British Dominions and the French Empire. In their hands was money enough to compete with any one of the big

Powers. In their names gold balances stood higher than the gold reserves of Britain and France together. Throughout the world they controlled vast commercial enterprises and for years their hands had pulled the strings behind the power politics which had made the war inevitable. Some had ostensibly claimed to be interested only in the restoration of Peace. To those Cartwright had first appealed.

And slowly their strength had grown.

Sibilla, who was Vania, had been bought.

Now they stood at the threshold of a victory which would double and redouble their wealth and their power. They could see nothing which could stop them. They had no country, no scruples, no patriotism, no concern for others. They were worshippers at the Shrine of Power—the Syndicate of Power.

And Sibilla led them.

They sat in front of Sibilla, in comfortable chairs, and it might have been the board meeting of an exceptionally affluent company. In the middle of the front row was a man older than most of the others—a gaunt scarecrow of an Englishman with white hair that stood upright from his head, baleful eyes, and a parchmentlike skin which suggested that he was even older than he was.

At one end of the room stood Cartwright.

The man looked pale and ill, and his hands were unsteady. He gave the impression that he had not slept for days. He saw men with whom he had worked, and whom he had trusted, members of that Syndicate of Power which was to crush his dreams. He hated them. Every man he hated—yet just behind him stood two uniformed officers of the Vanian Army.

There was a hum of conversation which stopped as Sibilla rose to his feet. He lifted a hand, and he started to speak in French—the language more universally understood than any other.

'Gentlemen, the ultimatums have been delivered, and the time-limit expires at six o'clock this evening—less than nine hours from now. Each country affected has seen a demonstration of our Power, and there is little-doubt of immediate acquiescence. We shall doubtless have isolated instances of insurrection when the fuller demands are made clear, but nothing is likely to be serious, except...'

He paused.

Had Loftus been watching he would have gained a sardonic amusement from the changes in the faces looking towards Sibilla. Practically every man there craned forward. Complacency and satisfaction disappeared—in some cases there was even alarm.

'What is it?' rasped the old man in the front row.

'A word from Cartwright's sister,' said Sibilla. 'She is in Venn, and due to arrive here at any moment. Since this meeting had been convened already I considered it wiser to discuss the matter with her in front of you all. She stated simply that she must talk with her brother about the lenses. She is bringing with her Cartwright's technical assistant.'

'Didn't know he had one!' growled the white-haired Englishman.

Sibilla swung round towards Cartwright.

'Did you?'

'Of course. Several.' The answer satisfied the members of the Syndicate of Power, and questions were flung at Sibilla from all sides. They referred mostly to the possibility of the Powers accepting the Vanian challenge. To all of them Sibilla gave reassuring answers, until the door nearest Sibilla opened, and a secretary stepped in.

'They have arrived, Excellency.'

'Bring them in at once.'

The man bowed and went out. There was a rustling of

movement, and every eye turned towards the door. The old man in the front row half-rose from his seat, to the annoyance of a fez-capped Turk behind him.

Then Garry Cartwright came in.

She glanced across at her brother, and her expression for a moment showed what she was feeling. Then she was cool and composed again, and stopped near Cartwright. At her side was another officer of the Vanian Army, and by the side of Bill Loftus as he entered were two men—both of them large. Sibilla proposed to take no chances with Cartwright's 'technician'.

And then the old man roared:

'Technician be damned, that's Loftus!'

The speaker was Professor Grafton!

'Loftus,' said Bill Loftus gently, and yet his voice carried through the large room. 'Good morning, Professor. I wondered whether you had been kidnapped or whether you had left by your own volition.'

'You damned fool!' roared Professor Grafton, and in that moment his daughter would not have recognised the man, for his face was twisted with hatred, and his pointing finger quivered towards Sibilla. 'This is Loftus, Department Z's chief agent!'

Sibilla snapped: 'He is quite harmless! Loftus, if...'

Loftus vaulted from the floor to the dais where Sibilla was standing and raised his empty hands above his head. Four automatics were trained on him while the Cartwrights stared and Grafton stood in front of the dais, his parchment-like face crimson with rage.

And *fear.*

* * *

It was not Loftus's size alone that gained him a hearing. There was something in his manner more impressive by far than Sibilla's, although the latter was dressed in the formal fashion that was his custom, while Loftus looked as if he had slept in his rumpled grey suit for nights on end. But there was silence in the room, and forty pairs of eyes were turned towards the big man, who looked about him and smiled—smiled as if he was sharing the best joke of all time.

'Gentlemen,' he said, 'I have nothing up my sleeve.'

Garry snorted.

Sibilla's face paled, and his eyes glittered angrily.

'Loftus, this is wasting time, and...'

'But I come,' Loftus steam-rollered on, 'as the representative of the Allied Governments.' He spoke with such conviction that it sounded true. 'Your demands were, of course, anticipated before Jonathan Scott returned to England.'

'Impossible!' snapped Sibilla.

'My dear Sibilla, credit the Secret Service with a little ability. We knew who had come here, and we knew when they were likely to leave. Cartwright's negotiations were allowed to proceed but not in the secrecy he imagined. Grafton's part in the affair has been well known for some time.'

'Then why didn't you act, you liar?' roared Grafton.

'We'll get to that,' said Loftus. 'Sibilla—what are your demands precisely?'

'If you need them repeated,' said Sibilla icily, 'they are the complete surrender of all arms and ammunition within a specified time. And understand that our planes can fly by night as if it were day, and that any attacking planes that might come from England or France can *be sighted* by night. There is no chance of your fleet escaping—nor the French.'

'Take the fool out and shoot him!' cried Grafton.

'I shouldn't,' said Loftus gently. 'I was searched for guns

and other things, but they allowed me to keep this.' He took a stout fountain-pen from his pocket and raised it—and his manner was so impressive that they stared, aghast.

'What is it?' demanded Sibilla.

'Nitro-glycerine,' said Loftus. 'An older invention than your lens, gentlemen, but effective. The pen is loaded with it. If I drop it on the floor now, or throw it towards the body of the audience, it will go off.' Loftus looked at Grafton with his head on one side. 'You will be good enough to confirm that, Professor? The ounce or two of nitro-glycerine in this pen will explode and completely wreck this room. And those in it,' he added as if regretfully.

'And *you*!' cried Grafton.

'And the Cartwrights,' admitted Loftus. 'A regrettable fact, gentlemen, but we will be prepared to make the sacrifice. After all, if the controlling geniuses of this remarkable syndicate are blown out of recognition, and Sibilla is destroyed, things will be at a standstill. Agents in Venn are waiting to hear the explosion and to advise the Allied Governments. The moment will be considered ripe for the attack on Vania, which Vania is not likely to withstand long. You do issue all instructions personally, don't you, Sibilla?'

There was a deathly silence in the big room. Loftus was able to see every man there, including the officers with their guns.

'You do, don't you?' he insisted.

'Of course he does!' Cartwright snapped the words. 'He was boasting to me today that he controls everything; the Navy and Air Force are waiting for word from him, and they won't move without it!'

'I'd hoped so,' said Loftus. 'You are holding the major Powers up, gentlemen—and I am holding you up in turn.

Don't imagine that I shall be unwilling to go out with the rest of you.'

There was another tense silence.

Garry Cartwright wanted to scream.

An officer raised his gun, as if he were going to shoot and chance the consequences. Loftus looked at him, and his voice was harsh.

'Turn about!'

The man hesitated, and Loftus lifted the pen. Sibilla snapped an order, and the man turned round.

'Hold your gun behind you,' Loftus snapped.

Again the man obeyed, and Loftus bent down quickly—so quickly that there was a gasp from the men gathered there, for the fountain-pen seemed to drop from his fingers. Loftus straightened up with the gun in his hand.

'Get the others, Garry. Help her, Cartwright.'

'But...' an officer protested.

'Get them!' snapped Loftus, 'or by God I'll...'

He raised the pen above his head, and a man in the middle of the crowd exclaimed on a high-pitched note, and then collapsed on his chair. The officers removed their guns so quickly that in different circumstances it would have seemed comic—and the Cartwrights collected them.

'Did you order the demonstration of the lens, Sibilla?' asked Loftus.

'Ye-es.'

'The sinking of ships by night, the bombing of men by night?'

'It was necessary!'

'It was mass murder,' said Loftus, 'worse because there was no declaration of war. Cartwright, has he got the formula for the lens?'

'No. It's in my head,' Cartwright said slowly. 'They can't

make more without me, but they've got enough to last them for years. There's a factory here busy on the construction of it. I put the final touches in person.'

'That's all right,' said Loftus, and he looked at Sibilla. 'You know what happens to murderers?'

'No, no!' shrieked Sibilla. 'You can't...'

Loftus fired.

There was no pity in him, and he took that life without a moment's compunction. He shot for the forehead, and the bullet found its mark. There was a spreading hole as Sibilla slowly collapsed, and a scream from the audience, while a dozen men jumped to their feet.

Loftus looked down on them, and his lips curled.

'That was Sibilla,' he said. 'No orders will be effective in Vania until there is a properly constituted Government—that's a disadvantage of dictatorships. Garry, go round and get their names—if any man lies he'll be treated as Sibilla was treated.'

He waited there, while the Cartwrights collected names.

They were flying back to England forty-eight hours after the triumph. In that time many things had happened. A Government had been formed hastily in Vania, Sibilla had been disowned, the ships watching the Seven Seas had been recalled—for without the factory and without the one man who knew how to make the lens Vania could not win through. The Syndicate of Power had been arrested to a man, for they had not escaped from the Senate House. Each of the four big Powers concerned had agreed to the re-establishment of Vanian neutrality, and the Syndicate was to be tried by a neutral Court. Loftus knew that in all likelihood the members would be imprisoned for the duration of the War; he would have preferred a more decisive punishment.

Grafton had talked.

He had failed to find the lens, although he had got close to it. His nearness had earned the interest of Forster and then Cartwright. Edward Grey had known what was hanging on to the success or failure of his experiments, and had financed him for that reason—Grey, also, was a member of the Syndicate.

Grafton had staged the scene at the Cliff Royal to impress the Errols—even to collapse, and Janice had backed him up and yet been frightened of what might happen, of what he was doing. She had believed in Warncliffe and suspected her father of double-dealing. Even Grey had not known that Grafton, on the strength of his discoveries, had earned a place on the Syndicate—meaning to come out on the credit side whether he made the discovery or failed.

The kidnapping had been staged.

Paul had been a member of Cartwright's organisation, and blackmailing Warncliffe because of the latter's double-crossing. That the gangs organised by Forster and by Cartwright had been located by the police, and those against whom there was no specific charge would be interned. Cartwright's men had all been actuated by the same ideal as Cartwright: Peace at all cost.

He knew that Cartwright had staged the disappearance of the bodies of Horley and Wilson from the Manor, to impress Loftus—in the vain hope of shaking the Department off. He knew that Cartwright and Forster had been watching each other, and that the Waterloo dago and the man who had been shot outside the Brook Street flat had been Forster's men—'executed' on Cartwright's orders. Horley and Wilson had cheated and defrauded the Government—and Horley had given away information about Craigie and his men—and Cartwright had had them killed, while emptying the safes of all important documents with a view to having a stronger hold on the

British Government, another weapon in the drive for 'Peace'.

Internationally, the situation was 'as you were'.

An International Neutral Commission under the auspices of the League of Nations would dismantle the Vanian ships and aircraft fitted with the lens, and the invention would disappear as a practical weapon in the present war. It could not have ended more satisfactorily, Loftus considered, now that Cartwright was dead and the British Government could not get the secret of the lens.

As he had started the flight back to England he had gone through much of it in his mind, and with Garry. The one thing which had puzzled him was the two-headed disc—and when Garry had explained it he had laughed for the first time that day. For it was a Vanian coin, long since out of circulation, and worth a ha'-penny. In the affair of the Syndicate of Power it had meant nothing.

'So many things do,' said Loftus. 'It's a matter of sorting the wheat from the chaff, my sweet.'

And after that they had been silent until they had talked of Cartwright, and he had added:

'And now we've got to talk about you.'

'What about me?' asked Garry dispassionately. 'I've tried, and I've failed. I've been a party to killing, and motives don't matter—and I can't say I care.'

'Could anyone make you care?' asked Loftus.

'What do you mean?'

'I was thinking of Mark Errol.'

'What's the use?' she asked dully.

And then she told him that she had seen Errol months before, and had known what she felt about him. It was why she had been at Waterloo, for she had wanted to make sure that Forster's man did not kill the Errols, particularly Mark;

Forster had wanted to teach the Department a salutary lesson, and the syndicate had learned of it through Warncliffe.

'So he did something worth while,' said Loftus. 'Garry, sit back and hold tight. No one but a few of our fellows has ever seen you. No one can identify you as Cartwright's sister. He'll never be on trial, and the Press will never have this story in full—trust the Ministry of Information for that. All you have to do is to change your name—and let Mark know where to find you.'

She leaned forward, a hand gripping his wrist tightly.

'You *mean* that?'

'I can't see,' said Loftus, 'why you should suffer from those ideals, Garry.'

A fortnight later, Mark Errol applied to Craigie for a fortnight's leave of absence—and got it. Loftus knew that he had heard from Garry. On that night Mike Errol and Davidson, Oundle, Thornton and the others were gathered together in Loftus's flat, for the invalids had recovered and there was little to do. If Mike had a complaint it was that his cousin had deserted him.

'Stop moaning,' ordered Ned Oundle as he sprawled back on a settee. 'He might have fallen for that large woman who wanted to marry the Professor. The one with the Freud complex.'

'And he might not,' said Mike with spirit. 'Once an Errol always an Errol and possessed of the best of taste. And that reminds me, didn't you have a Talbot once?'

'I got it back,' said Ned cheerfully.

'You even got your voice back, which is a disadvantage,' said Bill Loftus. 'And it's time you fellows cleared out. I want some sleep.'

He did not want to sleep, however.

He wanted to think, and Oundle—who shared the flat—

knew it, and joined the others in an onslaught on a respectable club whose older members considered that the young men out of uniform should be ashamed of themselves. While Loftus sat back in an easy-chair and thought of many things, including Forster and Paul, who had been shot, and Cartwright who had died with his ideals, and Grafton who had deserved to die but would live, and Janice Grafton—who had gone to stay with relatives whom he hoped would understand, and Mark and Garry...

When Oundle got back in the early hours, Loftus was fast asleep in his chair, and Oundle tiptoed past him.

ABOUT THE AUTHOR

John Creasey, born in 1908, was a paramount English crime and science fiction writer who used myriad pseudonyms for more than six hundred novels. He founded the UK Crime Writers' Association in 1953. In 1962, his book *Gideon's Fire* received the Edgar Award for Best Novel from the Mystery Writers of America. Many of the characters featured in Creasey's titles became popular, including George Gideon of Scotland Yard, who was the basis for a subsequent television series and film. Creasey died in Salisbury, UK, in 1973.

DEPARTMENT Z

FROM OPEN ROAD MEDIA

OPEN ROAD
INTEGRATED MEDIA

Find a full list of our authors and
titles at www.openroadmedia.com

FOLLOW US
@OpenRoadMedia